T0029511

the names of the things that were there

Selection and foreword by
Juan Villoro

OTHER PRESS
NEW YORK

the
names
of the
things
that were
there

STORIES

Antonio Skármeta

Translated from the Spanish by Curtis Bauer

Originally published in Spanish as *Los nombres de las cosas que allí había*
in 2019 by Penguin Random House Grupo Editorial, S.A.
Copyright © Antonio Skármeta, 2019
Foreword copyright © Juan Villoro, 2019
Translation copyright © Curtis Bauer, 2023

Production editor: Yvonne E. Cárdenas
Text designer: Jennifer Daddio
This book was set in Baskerville by
Alpha Design & Composition of Pittsfield, NH

1 3 5 7 9 10 8 6 4 2

Library of Congress Cataloging-in-Publication Data
Names: Skármeta, Antonio, author. | Bauer, Curtis, 1970- translator. |
Villoro, Juan, 1956- editor of compilation, writer of foreword.
Title: The names of the things that were there : stories / Antonio Skármeta ;
translated from the Spanish by Curtis Bauer ; selection and foreword
by Juan Villoro.
Other titles: Nombres de las cosas que allí había. English
Description: New York : Other Press, [2023] | Originally published in
Spanish as Los nombres de las cosas que allí había in 2019
by Penguin Random House Grupo Editorial, S.A.
Identifiers: LCCN 2023000608 (print) | LCCN 2023000609 (ebook) |
ISBN 9781635420760 (paperback ; acid-free paper) | ISBN 9781635420777 (ebook)
Subjects: LCSH: Skármeta, Antonio—Translations into English. |
LCGFT: Short stories.
Classification: LCC PQ8098.29.K3 N6613 2023 (print) |
LCC PQ8098.29.K3 (ebook) | DDC 863/.64—dc23/eng/20230201
LC record available at https://lccn.loc.gov/2023000608
LC ebook record available at https://lccn.loc.gov/2023000609

As soon as I was
on top of the rock,
I stood up and called out
all the names
of the things
that were there.

ANTONIO SKÁRMETA

contents

a man of principles

JUAN VILLORO

Literary vocation belongs to the rarities of the world. Suddenly, a girl's or a young man's mind is filled with birds that they don't know how to situate; some undefined thing seeks to take flight and scatters, staining the sun with mercurial flapping. That impulse is usually a result of an absence, the many voids that define adolescent life, but it also comes from some external stimulus, from what a friend said, a luminous verse in the middle of a book, a melody that demands to be sung and sung again and again.

Antonio Skármeta's stories tackle the uncanniness of literary initiation. *Enthusiasm*, the book that brought him initial recognition in 1967, is pierced by one essential question: How to make art out of one's life? "The Young Man with the Story," which opens this collection, is about a kid who wants to write. To do this, he isolates himself in a run-down shack on a beach; his solitude is supposed to trigger his creativity. In a state of philosophical plenitude, he claims: "I know how to be a man who stays still." However, his real impulse to write comes from his unexpected contact with other people, from a fear that gradually becomes a feeling of solidarity. When something finally occurs to him it is a consequence of having lived it already. At the age of twenty-seven Skármeta, in his unmistakable way, reveals how experience is translated into imagination, the elusive material we use to create literature.

Another story from the same book, "Among All Things, the First Is the Sea," describes a writer in a state of larval development. His life is a siesta of sorts before his final awakening. He doesn't seem to have much going for him, but he trusts the sea.

Skármeta demonstrates proof of his authority in *Enthusiasm*. One story from this book serves as a kind of emotional portfolio. In "Cinderella in San Francisco" (not included in this collection), not only is the main character a newcomer, but so is the country he comes from. A woman from the United States asks how many people can fit in Chile. The first-person narrator says eight million, adding that this population is missing the best thing, and the following dialogue ensues:

"Are they sad, by any chance? Aren't they happy?"
"They aren't happy," I said.
"Why?"
"Because they're never happy."
"Why?"
"Because they're just starting out, that's why."

In a letter to a friend, the Mexican poet Carlos Pellicer wrote: "I'm twenty-three years old and I think the world is the same age as I am." Skármeta's stories are shaped by an identical conviction: the nation, the sea, the sun, one's profession, all are things that are beginning. With Adamic intention, the protagonist of "The Young Man with the Story" says: "As soon as I was on top of the rock, I stood up and called out all the names of the things that were there." The surroundings are baptized as if they were just coming into existence. The narrator does not know what will happen, but he wants to describe it. Through this exhilarating approach, he turns his uncertainty into expertise. On the verge of beginning, he discovers the beauty of not being sure of anything.

In "Public Relations," the rite of passage refers to a turning point, a crucial situation: the transition from hatred to affection. An obligatory physical rivalry is transformed into a voluntary emotional bond of complicity.

By the time his second book, *Naked on the Roof,* won the 1969 Casa de las Américas Prize, Skármeta had already mastered two fundamental stylistic techniques: his stories had rapid plots that led to an inevitable denouement, and his lyrical prose gave the story above all else an opportunity for metaphors to reach hallucinatory proportions.

"The Cyclist from San Cristóbal," "To the Sands," and "Basketball" belong to the first category, but they include rapturous passages where language runs amok. The cyclist pedals in sensual defiance of the cosmos: "And from that last surge that came from the soles of my feet filling my thighs and hips and chest and neck and forehead with beautiful, boisterous, hot blood, from a crowning, from my body's assault against God, from an irresistible course, I felt the slope easing for a second and I opened my eyes and looked directly into the sun." Reading Chekhov, Hemingway, and Saroyan, Skármeta learned to make use of essential plotlines, but he also incorporated moments of poetic "madness" into them. If some of Cortázar's best stories are located in the region of a threshold, where the verifiable brushes against the fantastic, Skármeta, who dedicated his master's thesis to the Argentine writer, rarefies reality in another way, endowing it with poetic elation.

Those of us who were beginning to write at the tail end of the last century saw him as a young guru. There's nothing better for an apprentice than a master who is obsessed with the art of beginning.

The first sentence in the book *Naked on the Roof* (1969) established Skármeta as an expert in beginnings: "Besides, it was my birthday." I didn't know that a story could start in medias res. The action has already started and the reader "interrupts" it. That puzzling first line aroused my curiosity: Besides what? What could have happened before that?

In 1973 I highlighted this passage in Skármeta's third book, *Free Throw*: "I think: when I grow up I'm going to know what to say in these situations; I'm going to have a mouth full of words; I'll stop crouching like a cat, pawing through books and shadows." The narrator is referring to the difficulty of revealing his feelings to a girl. I guess I identified with that challenge, but also with the desire that the future would give me the eloquence I didn't have at that time.

Skármeta's young people are blank pages, drafts of themselves, prologues of lives to come. There will be words in the future. The paradox is that those who have nothing to say are masterfully narrated. The characters' stuttering is the narrator's eloquence.

A PERSONAL DOSSIER

Reading a writer who is an authority figure on *beginning* is pivotal for a future writer. I draw on my own autobiographical testimony to better understand the impact that Skármeta had in the late sixties and early seventies on the Latin American literary scene. I turned fifteen in 1971, and my best friend recommended a self-help manual that was essential reading for seducing girls and surviving the restrictive world of grown-ups: the novel *In Profile*, by José Agustín. The plot was set in a middle-class neighborhood very similar to my own, and the protagonist's predicaments were the same ones I was afraid to admit to myself. An inner mirror that reflected desires, anxieties, and lost opportunities. I understood, for the first time and forever after, that the main character in literature is the reader.

No book had ever included me like that. This revelation prompted me to tell my best friend while we were riding on a streetcar one day: "I'm going to become a writer." He looked at me as if I had told him I was going to rob a bank or become the first Mexican astronaut. Up to that moment, my main interests had been rock music, television, stories about soccer, and comics. The plunge into literature seemed like a daring feat similar in danger to those human cannonballs who were flying around in circuses at the time.

Reading the newspaper *Excélsior*, I discovered that the National Autonomous University was offering a free short-story workshop, and I decided to apply. I had written a story, but only one. One Wednesday, at seven in the evening, I went up to the tenth floor of the Rectory Tower. All the lights were out except one. Under its triangular glow, the Ecuadorian Miguel Donoso Pareja was reviewing manuscripts. In *The Savage Detectives* Roberto Bolaño immortalized the workshops of the poet Juan Bañuelos, who met on Tuesdays in the same place. José Alfredo Zendejas attended both workshops; José would assume the poetic alias of Mario Santiago Papasquiaro and would enter fiction as Ulises Lima, the rebellious reality scholar who stars in *The Savage Detectives*. I was the youngest in the workshop, and Zendejas took me under his wing. He asked me about my favorite poets, appraised my sincere

ignorance, and resolved to educate me. Donoso
Pareja, meanwhile, asked me how many stories I'd
written. "Two," I replied, to sound as if I was prolific.
"Bring them next week," the teacher suggested; he
had just published the anthology *Prosa joven de América
hispana*, but he didn't seem very confident about having such a young student in his workshop.

I wrote a second story in a hurry; it was set in a
mine (an entirely unfamiliar subject). I had the naïve
desire to support the working class through my prose.
With mistaken benevolence, Donoso Pareja attributed
this story to an "earlier" stage (as if, at fifteen, I could
have an earlier stage!) and believed that the other
story (the first one I had written) indicated that I could
dispense with those defects. So, I was accepted into
the workshop.

The Latin American novel was at that time a
dilated form of complexity. Vargas Llosa's *Conversation
in the Cathedral*, Carpentier's *The Recourse to the Method*,
Roa Bastos's *I The Supreme*, Fuentes's *A Change of Skin*,
Márquez's *The Autumn of the Patriarch*, and Cortázar's
Rayuela regarded literature as a voracious and erudite
experiment. It wasn't easy to emulate such excessive
creativity.

The "boom" generation brought literature to the center of cultural and political discussion, and made front-page news in the papers. It also had a "trawling" effect, the general public becoming intrigued by authors from the previous generation, those who were more concerned with writing than with proclaiming the novelty of their writing. Onetti, Rulfo, Borges, Bioy Casares, Felisberto Hernández became my tutelary gods, along with the short-story writer Cortázar. In my own muddled way, I tried to merge my passions for the countercultural with threshold literature, where realism bordered on the fantastic. "You have to read Skármeta," Donoso Pareja told me; he had included the Chilean author in his anthology. As usual, José Alfredo Zendejas (aka Mario Santiago) had beaten me to the punch. He already knew of the author and endorsed the recommendation.

In 1976 I won second place in a short-story contest sponsored by the university magazine *Punto de partida*. Roberto Bolaño won third place in poetry in the same contest. Poli Délano, the Chilean short-story writer exiled in Mexico, was one of the jurors, and he noticed Skármeta's influence in my story. At the awards ceremony cocktail party, Poli and I were talking about it when Bolaño approached us. He joined the conversation and, with his passionate fondness for extremes, regretted having been awarded a prize ("if anything I deserve a reprimand") and praised Skármeta, comparing him to the great Russian writers.

Many years later, Rodrigo Fresán and I talked with Bolaño about the relationship between Skármeta's story "To the Sands" and *The Savage Detectives*. In both texts a Mexican and a Chilean set off "on the road," determined to embark upon their poetic examination of the world. In "To the Sands," the main characters sell their blood so they can go to a jazz show. In order to deserve art, one must live accordingly, understanding that breathing and chomping and screaming and spitting can be poetic acts. Whoever accepts the risks of moving along the thin line that separates madness from inspiration, and dares to sacrifice his blood, is already a living poet, even if he has not yet produced a work of art.

As usual, Roberto disagreed with us. ("Why are you always contradictory?" the journalist Mónica Maristain asked him. "I never contradict," Bolaño answered humorously, denying the assertion and confirming it at the same time.) By then, he had already distanced himself from his former passion for

Skármeta, and, like every author, he modified the lineage to which he wanted to belong. But the similarities are there, and they help clarify the cultural atmosphere in which Fresán began writing in Argentina, Bolaño in Chile, and I in Mexico.

"PANIC HAS NO SOUND"

Like Onetti, Skármeta stops action to linger on a significant gesture. He doesn't limit himself to describing a mannerism or expression; he charges it with metaphors to transform it into a kind of parable. The story "First Year, Elementary," which appears in *Free Throw*, narrates the parting between two brothers. The elder leaves home, contrary to his parents' wishes. He earns his destiny, but he's about to lose someone he loves to his brother. The goodbye is narrated in the following way:

> *I look into his eyes and feel my neck sagging, my teeth*
>   *gleaming.*
> *Something stops my brother then.*
> *He stands there for a moment with his hands empty*
>   *and ambitious, his arms full of air, like a windmill*
>   *without wind, like a ship without water.*

The younger brother is suddenly a predatory animal whose teeth are "gleaming." He will stay with the girl, keep the life the other leaves behind. The young man who has decided to leave is ambitious, but he has very little at his disposal; "his hands empty" and "his arms full of air" reflect his precariousness, but also his courage. The destiny of the one who is leaving and the destiny of the one who stays behind are encapsulated in that last embrace.

The general tone of *Free Throw*, the author's third book of short stories, is very much reminiscent of Italian neorealist cinema. Scenes of brittle sentimentality inside the family unit, framed by historical events that affect the characters, are where objects and "insignificant" gestures acquire transcendent meanings.

"First Year, Elementary" and "Fish" take place in immigrant homes. Both stories underscore the importance of blood ties for those who come from some faraway place. The true welcoming homeland is the house where they live. The same driving force is at work in these stories: in a hard-won home, someone wants to leave. As I have already mentioned, "First Year, Elementary" is about the first-born son's escape, the son who already finds those walls suffocating; "Fish" is about a singular escape of two grandparents, still capable of an adventure that will take them to the ends of the earth; that is, around the block.

"Ballad for a Fat Man," which introduces a future protagonist of the novel *I Dreamed the Snow Was Burning*, addresses one of the most difficult issues to control in short fiction: political education.

The novel is a voluntarily "imperfect" genre, which alters and questions its structure, and it opens spaces to discuss different versions of the world. The terrorists in Dostoyevsky's *The Demons* or the critics of modernity in Huxley's *Counterpoint* expose their convictions in long *tertulias*, or conversations, during which the overall plot is suspended. The story can't allow itself such pauses; everything in it depends on following a story that, as Horacio Quiroga longed for, moves with the crisp precision of an arrow.

There are not many great political stories, but Skármeta has written some highly unique ones. "Ballad for a Fat Man" reflects the climate in the political party Unidad Popular, the social polarization during those days, the uncertainty of the times to come. Set against the backdrop of the reforms undertaken by Salvador Allende's government, the story begins in a twentieth-century setting similar to the agora in classical Greece: the courtyard of a school. The story goes on to recount a process of ideological maturation and ends in a confrontation where affection is challenged by beliefs: the friends from a different time embody two different versions of the left. The story leaves off when they can become either accomplices or enemies. Skármeta doesn't take sides; instead, tragically, Chile's history found a way to wipe out those possibilities for the future.

It's difficult to gauge the effects that exile had on an author who, perhaps because he was a descendant of Croatian immigrants, had a unique sense of belonging. Interestingly enough, several stories in his first three books celebrate the local microcosm and at the same time suggest abandoning it. A stimulating contradiction guides his characters. Leaving Antofagasta, discovering Santiago, traveling the world are rewards that involve loss. His characters allow themselves to be captivated by some terrifying possibility; they love the cracks on their street, but understand that there is nothing as valuable as leaving, and they leap into the unknown, prepared to risk the consequences.

Exile changed this situation. "Man with a Carnation in His Mouth" represents an initial reaction to the author's new circumstances. The young woman who is the protagonist of the story has just endured a political tragedy, the coup d'état in Chile, and finds herself in Lisbon in the midst of a hopeful situation, the commemoration of the night of the Carnation Revolution, in which the left triumphed. There she meets a young Portuguese man who is celebrating the end of the fascist regime by holding a carnation between his teeth. When he learns that the young woman is from Chile, he understands that it is too soon for her to say goodbye to all the malice in the world. The story brings together the essential themes of exile, love, and politics, and it foreshadows the narrative sobriety that Skármeta will acquire far from Chile. The lyrical passages that previously dominated entire stories ("Blue Days for an Anchor" in *Enthusiasm*, "Turned Over in the Air" in *Naked on the Roof*), or emerged as poetic outbursts in more realistic plots, disappear from his horizon.

A remarkable example of "new journalism" is "From Blood to Oil," which tells the story of a terrorist attack at Fiumicino Airport. A real event told with the subjective force of fiction. As in "Ballad for a Fat Man" or "Man with a Carnation in His Mouth," everyday life in this short story is altered by the fractures of History. As a consequence of their fear and the bullets, the passengers gathered in a waiting room are reduced to a single body struggling to survive. Individual destiny becomes dramatically collective. A glass wall shatters as a symbol of a broken world. What is most surprising, however, is not the violent disruption of routine, but the unsettling possibility of returning to it. Nothing is resolved, but life goes on. From the spilled blood we move on to the oil that drives and normalizes destinies...and destinations.

Skármeta's incursion into screenwriting, television, and novels distanced him from the genre that he seemed called to cultivate with greater skill in his youth. It would seem that he also lost his first literary love when he lost his country. *Ardiente paciencia*, retitled *The Postman* in English, began as a radio play and was successively transformed into a stage play, a film (directed by Skármeta himself), and a novel, which in turn gave rise to another film, *Il Postino*, which was nominated for an Oscar for Best Picture, and an opera starring Plácido Domingo. A "stateless" text, to use Julio Ramón Ribeyro's expression, *The Postman* required many territories of arrival or origin. From that point on, Skármeta became "first and foremost" the author of this story that brought him immense international success. Fame, as we know, is a simplification. The spotlights that shined on Neruda and his letter carrier left other aspects of Antonio Skármeta in shadow.

Freedom of Movement, a collection of short stories written over several years and set in different countries, appeared in 2015. I have chosen two stories from this collection. Both address the subject of the double. One of them announces the subject in its title: "Borges." To assuage his loneliness, the protagonist travels to Paris, eager to follow in the footsteps of a friend who lives there. In the city that displays itself as an adventure of order—never noticed by its troubled inhabitants—he discovers that his potential host is going through a crisis. Stepping into the shoes of another can signify either vicarious bliss or the reiteration of ruin.

"Teresa Clavel's Lover" recycles the theme in a different way: every hero requires a witness; to enhance the facts, someone, by necessity, must be "the other." Celebrity is maintained by the anonymity of others. The story moves forward like a fine-tuned machine and leads to a plot of romantic and political intrigue in Haiti.

In his early writing, Skármeta presented departure as a complex challenge. In *Freedom of Movement* he moves with the ease of someone accustomed to

relocation, although he privileges the geography of nowhere, the non-places, to locate the core of the action:
a highway, a chain hotel, a seaside resort, a mundane
middle-class apartment.

Skármeta's stories rarely appear without musical
quotations and references. It wouldn't be a surprise or
an exaggeration if this collection were accompanied
by a CD. Even in front of the imminent horror in
"From Blood to Oil," the author is reminded of a melody. Silence comes only when you are on the brink of
paralysis. There the narrator understands that "panic
has no sound." The "pain of the world" (*Weltschmerz*)
drove young Werther to suicide. To overcome this
emptiness, you have to speak out, turn up the volume
of a melody, put roosters on the pages. Skármeta
slammed the door when he entered literature, ready to
make some noise.

Some writers refrain from sharing their hobbies
and prefer to concentrate on those of their characters, which they don't always share. Like Cortázar,
Skármeta brings his readers into a nightclub where
music lovers gather and mentions Lucho Gatica,
Petula Clark, or Ella Fitzgerald. The style of his first
three books has a lot of swing and jazz, a score shaken
by wind that blows only in the south of the planet,

where it seems like everything comes to an end, but where fishermen, miners, and poets prove that the place exists and they make it sparkle.

"We were the sun's chosen ones / And we didn't realize it," Vicente Huidobro wrote. In 1967, a Chilean storyteller understood that there is nothing as important as starting, and he turned that impulse into an aesthetic. A language was beginning, a country was beginning, a world was beginning: life was up ahead.

And this time, the chosen ones would notice: "I opened my eyes and looked directly into the sun."

the names of the things that were there

the young man with
the story

That's the house," Ernesto said. "A real palace. What do you think?"

I adjusted the backpack on my shoulders and could feel myself falling into a kind of rapture, a temperature rising from my gut to my eyes, coloring them with the intensity of my enthusiasm, with the urge to rush to the beach and run across the sand until I couldn't run anymore, and I could already imagine how doing that was going to fill me with laughter. "All the blue realm of the earth conquered for mankind." Not even a little wind, the white sand, the rocks cleverly distributed, and sky and sea enough to exhaust you, and my powerful throat, energetic, concocting words of praise, mute at that moment because any word would be everything, and a finger pointing to the horizon, escaping from my right hand, incomprehensible, telling a certain story at its own risk, one that I couldn't translate, and the dismayed expression on my face, and the hot sweat on my cheeks, and Ernesto smiling as he looked at me, magnanimous owner of the world, asking me what I thought, kindly enjoying my veneration of the earth, rubbing his hands together, pretending to chew on something, opening and closing his mouth with just enough air, never ceasing to look at me, never ceasing to smile.

"Extraordinary," I replied. "Call me 'the King' from now on."

I talk like this, a little bit grandiose; there's nothing we can do about that.

"King of shit; on the third day you're gonna need to talk to someone, you'll feel like having some hot soup, or seeing some little *mujercita*; you'll head back down the road to Antofagasta."

"You don't know me," I replied, contemplating a squadron of pelicans flying over a gathering of rocks. I'd be perfectly capable of scorching myself on a rock without any regrets. I know how to be a man who stays still, God forgive me.

He picked up a regular-sized bag and dropped it on the sand.

"Here are your supplies. Canned food and beer. You'll find some wine inside the car. Don't drink too much."

"Don't worry," I told him. "I won't have time."

"You're not gonna have time? What are you planning to do?"

I replied with a theatrical gesture that was precisely imprecise; the truth was that I wanted to keep it to myself, that monologue that was surging inside me, with the same rhythm as my breathing, this new land I was seeing, the sudden maturity that had surfaced out of those tiresome days spent in Santiago, close to the end of my third year at the university, and that had directed my legs northward in a slow and peaceful journey across the pampas.

"Sleep," I answered. "Like a tired beast. Those university classes are tiring, you know?"

"I've heard that they wake you up," Ernesto said with astonishing astuteness.

I put my hand on his shoulder.

"Propaganda."

"But you get good grades, don't you?"

"Yes," I replied. "But that doesn't mean anything."

"What are you gonna do? Are you gonna drop out?"

"Thinking about it. I don't know. Maybe."

Ernesto scratched his head. I shrugged and held out my hand.

"Are you coming on Saturday?"

"Sure," he said. "Do you want me to carry the bag to the car?"

"No, leave it."

He reached into his right pocket and then handed me the keys.

"All right, King," he said, "have a good time."

"Don't worry," I replied.

I put the keys in my shirt pocket and picked up the bag of supplies. Then I smiled at Ernesto and slowly started walking to the structure. I heard the engine clattering and wished it would move away as soon as possible so I could feel the full extent of the silence of the place and begin to hear my voice, finally, ignorantly answering the silent questions I was asking myself, taking in the salty ocean smells on the walls of my nostrils. All at once the sound of the motor died out and a bullet blast jolted my entire being. I immediately turned in the direction of the car. Ernesto was about a hundred meters away, waving his arms in the air and motioning for me to wait for him.

I was nervous as I ran toward him, and as he rushed up to me, waving a revolver in his right hand.

When we caught up to each other he flopped down on the sand.

"What's wrong?" I asked. "Did you fire the gun?"

"Yes. Take it."

I grabbed the gun with my left hand. It was heavier than I had imagined.

"I almost forgot to give it to you," he said.

I looked at the revolver and cautiously moved it to my other hand, careful to keep my fingers away from the trigger.

"Is it loaded?"

"It has five bullets in it," he said, picking at some gunk that had blown into his eye.

"What do you want me to do with it?" I asked. I held it out for him so he could take it back.

"Keep it."

"What for? I've never shot a gun in my life."

Ernesto continued to struggle with his eye. The sun was shining in his face, so he raised one hand for shade and with the other he wiped the tears out of his watering eyes.

"You might need it," he said. "I think I got sand in my eye."

I set the revolver aside, knelt down, and grabbed his head.

"Open it."

He tried to open his eye but all that did was irritate it more. When he finally managed to hold it open a little longer, I blew several violent breaths into it; it was just like a hurricane.

"Seems like it's out," he said so I wouldn't fuck it up anymore.

He stood up. I reached for the gun and held out my hand, to give it back to him.

"Take it with you," I said. "The only things to shoot at here are pelicans. What good's it going to do me? Other than make me really nervous!"

"Keep it," he insisted. "There are a lot of people around here." I glanced around mockingly.

Next to the old railroad car where I would be staying was a small hut, and about a hundred meters away another car, painted red with a Chilean flag on a white flagpole.

"Yes," I said. "There are more people here than in Glasgow, Scotland."

I turned around to look in the direction Ernesto's index finger was pointing.

"Hills," I remarked. "A thousand bare and beautiful hills."

"You never know where people live," he said.

"I'm sure. How do they make a living?"

"Maybe they come down to fish early in the morning. Don't you think?"

I looked at the gun in my right hand.

"Anyway," I said, "show me how this thing works."

"Point it somewhere."

I aimed the gun at a rock.

"First hold it straight and then pull the trigger."

"It doesn't have a safety?"

"It's broken."

I closed one eye and touched the trigger with my finger. The gunshot rang like a shrill whistle in my ears, and my hand shook. I missed, and a pinch of sand rose up, like dust around the rock.

Ernesto laughed.

"Practice your aim," he said. "In case you have a big shoot-out, there's more ammunition in the house. If you see any Polacks, kill them."

"All right," I said. "In honor of your grandfather."

I walked the few meters over to the bags and picked them up, and I noticed the car leaving as I continued walking toward the house.

The first thing I did when I stepped inside was open all the doors and windows to cool the hot air inside the train car. It was a railroad car from the

Antofagasta-Bolivia line, one of the same ones I
had ridden in when I was a kid, and it still had two
wooden seats at one end and some clothes hooks on
the walls, and the luggage racks on top were now
crowded with magazines, jars, shirts and shoes,
half-empty cigarette boxes, empty bottles, all mixed
together in admirable disorder. The car was divided
by a plywood wall, and each compartment had three
cots, the same kind the militia used. In one of the
corners there was still a toilet, and despite the notice-
able efforts someone had made to remove them, a
multitude of scribbles and scrawls could still be read
with relative ease. Most of them looked like a family of
cholos, each of the Indians adorned with their genita-
lia and delicious curves drawn above the toilet's water
tank.

At the opposite end someone had placed a small
table covered by a cloth curtain, on which there were
two kerosene stoves, and judging by the jars of rice
and sugar, and by the salt, and by the orange peels on
the floor, it could quite easily be the kitchen. Once I'd
made a full inspection of the palace, I stretched out
on each of the beds, bouncing on them and testing
their qualities, until I chose one facing the beach that
impressed me with its softness and size, where I could

comfortably lay my six-foot-two-inch frame and rest for a moment, looking up at the air vents and whistling through my teeth at whatever I wanted.

"Here I am," I said to myself, "like a shitty king lying on this bed peacefully enjoying my banishment, ready for everything to pass me by without fazing me, with three good pencils in my pocket, and with this one remaining insight that I need nothing else from the world."

"Here I am," I said later, lowering my voice, "lying down like a sly dog waiting to recover from my exhaustion, enjoying the smell of sweat on my shirt, with nothing to do for ever and ever amen, slightly aroused but not with any desire for a woman, moving like that Chinese vase T. S. Eliot had, quietly in motion, not desiring and not not desiring, making a threshold for words, concentrating so that my insignificant revelations might become epiphanic, so that my demon wakes up and agrees with me and we fuck each other in an easy struggle tonight, with nothing disturbing the calm beginning of my prose, while the pages advance and this wretch that I am petulantly passes my hand in front of my face, like the filthy owner of the world that I know myself to be, bawling my eyes out with the happiness of being, with no wind capable of knocking me off my horse and too free to start writing now as if I were sick in the head.

"Let's see what the beach has in store for us," I said, getting up, "and don't let anything bother you, unless you feel like being bothered, and then don't let anything calm you, brother."

I put a hand over my eyes to shade them, and looking at the sun I calculated the time. It appeared to be something like five o'clock in the afternoon, so I was still going to have sunshine for quite a while. I walked stretching and yawning to within a few meters of the shore and throwing off my clothes I lay naked on the sand, immediately feeling the warmth of the sun on my face and belly. I had tucked my shirt, which I had tied into a bundle, under the back of my neck, so that it rested peacefully with all the comfort I could ask for. My eyes barely open, I watched the pelicans' wings flapping heavily, hovering over an area of water that seemed to be teeming with sardines, and I saw them swoop down suddenly, dive into the sea, and emerge into the air dripping with the fish clutched tightly in their beaks. There were about thirty of these birds circling about, and aided by the stillness of the ocean, the noise of their wings, beating against the still, shimmering air, could be heard vividly, like a kind of dry vibration that sounded like music. I also spotted other, smaller birds cutting through the air high above; I didn't know what they were called, but their entire movement was harmonious, and they didn't seem to be looking for food or wanting to catch fish, and they didn't seem to be going anywhere either, for all they did was turn in the same space, sometimes in a line, or in groups of four, and it could be that all they wanted was to be up there flying, because they did, because it was good for them, that was their life, to stay suspended in the air, gliding after they had fluttered enough to earn that serene transport of themselves, and perhaps joyful to be flying birds and useless, except for that flight, high up there, highlighted like a black mark prolonging itself in the color of the sky, dividing the sun, dividing it into hundreds of little suns, snatching from it, I imagined, its only depth, carrying its glow on their beak, slipping it over their black plumage, shaking it off with their sharp heads, and reintegrating it into the air to divide the air in its turn and place itself freely in space.

"This is what I am," I said, stroking my belly, still looking at the birds, riveted by their movements, oblivious to my name and to the world, quietly withdrawn, seizing me. "This is what I am. Space. I begin here and at the tip of those dirty, crooked toes on my feet I end. And this is what is given to me, and I can already begin to be grateful for it."

I ran my hand over my face, burning, rough to the touch, with a few grains of sand scratching my cheeks, and tried to thank the space around me, in the first language that came to mind.

The first thing I said was a kind of prayer mixing the Our Father who art in heaven with Neruda's odes and with some poems I wrote when I was a kid, all sprinkled with rude interjections, which I threw in just to make some racket in the giving of thanks, as if thinking that if someone heard them, he wouldn't take me for a saint or some cocked-hat poet. Then it occurred to me that the proper thing to do would be to ask for my space to be preserved, held in warranty, inviolable, in other words, yes by women, if it occurred to them to do so, though not through death or plagues or any such filth as that. Gently the sun began to nag at me, so I turned over, lying on my belly with my face resting on the right side, and gazing only at the nearest patch of sand I continued to string together my speech, carefully, trying to make it sound honest and convincing.

At that moment, invigorated by my supplication and inclined to the ambition of the sound of my words, a prayer murmured into the ear of the woman lying next to me, the only one, the chosen one, and invigorated by the sun at rest on my backside, and by the hot sand pressing against my belly, I raised my voice to complain about not having more than what I had, arguing against time, heaping insults upon it for its honest destruction, pleading against the law of gravity that doesn't lift you to the stars when you propel yourself lightly from a rock with a certain longing to go as high as possible, protesting against the word "possible," clamoring for its eradication from the dictionary, protesting against the absurd usurpation that one day will come thanks to the air that I will have magnanimously given back I hope to the universe every time I breathe in, the same bellicose air that I now threw like stones hitting the sand and making it jump, rise up, dislocating it from its natural order, and suddenly, before that kind of pain, the only thing left was this inheritance: seeing yourself turned into a squeaky, wet thing that would hurt you by looking at you, testifying there where your body announces its withdrawal that it is right there, on your ground, thanks to your

13

laborious education in the work of the world, all its
absurd pain and its joy, looking at you with those
weighty few kilos, making the denouncement that you
are there, better than the one you were, or else, there
itself, but definitely betrayed, turned around in front
of you, not accepting you, denying the world without
a word, silently dispatching the father and the mystery
to the same hell, freely choosing his death, no longer
breathing the night of childbirth, or retiring at the age
of twenty after having concluded his education at the
entrance to a whorehouse, without a single gesture,
without any falsehood, with hushed cunning, thinking
of faith, denying the feeling, shaking his head, withdrawing life like a feather that had landed on his hair:
so light or troublesome; or, years later, in the distance,
I will glimpse him through a window overlooking the
shore, lying on the sand, pondering the same questions,
I will see him touching himself, thinking about his
name, testing the answer by knocking up the woman
beside him listening to what he has to say, or perhaps
he remains still, and then I know my name and can go
to sleep in my bed leaving the windows open so that
the sea breeze soaks into my wrinkles, shaping them
and exhausting them, leaving me mute with the taste
of fermented salt on my cheekbones.

I dug my fingers and toes into the earth as I bent
my knees and elbows, feeling the fine drizzle of sand
tickling the back of my neck, and I dragged my
forehead across it in a movement of denial, drawing
a sort of semicircle in the sand. I started speeding up
all these movements, involuntarily, without intend-
ing to, until it seemed that all the heat in the world
surrendered to me and that coals were piling up and
rotating, pulsating in my brain, and in my thighs, and
in my spine especially. I clung to the earth by squeezing a seashell with my right hand and keeping still; I
allowed myself to circulate freely through my veins
and then violently out into the rest of the space, feeling
the wet sensation on my stomach, chest, and neck,
snorting loudly, hands outstretched now, arms long at
the same time, like a crucified man, still digging the
earth with my forehead, eyes tightly pinched shut and
smiling.

When everything was over, I remained in the same
position for a moment longer, contemplating what
had happened, waiting for my breathing to recover
its proper rhythm, and patting the hair on my chest
with curiosity. Once things were in order, I turned
over, yawning and content. I lay on my back, and the
sudden opening of my eyes and the direct sunlight,

which I hadn't looked at for at least half an hour, hitting them, blinded me and forced me to close them for a while. I wiped away my tears with the palms of my hands, and when I finally managed to look out across the beach, I couldn't help but stretch myself to manifest the state of satisfaction that was growing inside me as I contemplated the sea, now absolutely serene, except for the bright sun on the water, which produced a barely perceptible kind of movement, the motionless birds on the rocks with their beaks scanning the horizon, squawking wildly, as if engaged in a discussion about the vastness that ordered the world in those blues through which the sun was beginning to enter.

When I stepped into the water, the first thing I did was immerse myself up to my knees, and I cleaned my stomach with my right hand, and then I cleaned my chest, and I sprinkled, spreading all my fingers at once, refreshing drops of water onto my face. I cupped water in my hand, raised it over my head, and then released it, letting it fall on my hair, as if I were baptizing myself, and when I said my name, Antonio, I noticed that it was not strange to me, that I would obey myself if I called myself by name like that, and during all the time that I kept pouring water on my head and repeating my name, the image of myself

repeating my name and pouring water on my head
appeared to me, only I, whom I imagined, was seriously looking at the horizon, with a kind of headache
that began to bother me, while the image seemed to
be laughing at everything, and it occurred to me that
he had just taken off his tailcoat, tidied his pants on
the lavender-scented sand, and, without picking up the
chips won at the casino, had gone to swim in the sea,
to ask without being dramatic, but in fact with joy,
what his name was on this earth.

I knew that by swimming I would get my body
used to the temperature of the water, so I emerged
from my first dive and quickly thrashed my arms
about, splashing noisily, spinning aimlessly, doing all
kinds of violent-mannered maneuvers. When I felt like
I was master of the sea, I swam slowly toward a large
rock that loomed a hundred meters away, my movements harmonious, balanced, spitting the salt water
that entered through my half-open mouth to the sides,
mostly with my eyes closed, opening them from time
to time to make sure that I continued in a straight
line, concerned about my cenesthesia, about the
contrast between my head, aching, and the magnificent state of internal strength in the rest of my body,
its comfortable half tension, the clarity with which its

lungs processed the air as it swam, and the dialogue
it engaged in with the ocean as it waved its arms,
pushing the water aside, pushing it to the shore like a
conquistador sighting new land.

As soon as I was on top of the rock, I stood up
and called out all the names of the things that were
there, in a loud, melodic voice, repeating the ones I
liked best, such as mountain, shore, seagull, pelican,
truth, and others like that, until I said "crab," without
there being a single crab in the vicinity, just to "cheat
a little," because I liked the word, or perhaps because
I wished that a crab would indeed appear, but I'd
hardly finished saying the word when one appeared
next to my left foot. Then I remembered a certain
book; I smirked as I stooped to pick the crustacean up,
and though my lips and my eyes and my whole body
were watching the critter kick, somehow I knew that
all the world's vanity, and that of Ecclesiastes, and all
the mighty vanity that will wisely one day come had
gotten into my very bones, because when I smirked
at the crab, somehow I knew that I was looking up.
I pierced it with a piece of wood that was floating
nearby, and I swam slowly back to the beach with the
crab skewered like that, trailing the swaying of my
right arm that was carrying it, still struggling to live,

as if invigorated by the sudden agitations in the water caused by the movements of my stroke.

I put my clothes on without drying off and walked to the train car. It was starting to get dark and my headache, which had already announced itself by that time, became more piercing. My lips felt dry and the images inside my head appeared as if placed under the light off orange reflectors, flashing, and much more painful if I closed my eyes. I felt my first shiver before I reached the door. I put my hand to my forehead, checking to see if I had a fever, but my hand felt as hot as my head. I went into the train car cursing my bad luck, buttoning up my shirt, and shaking my body to avoid the kind of icy currents that made it vibrate now and again. And I got even angrier when I saw the open notebooks on the table, and the three pencils on the blank sheets of paper, very neat and sharpened, and the desire to write that I had carried with me grew, but rabidly, annoying me, the same way I would have taken a club to kill a lurking mosquito. I closed the notebooks, sprawled out on the bed, and decided to look out the window until everything became absolutely dark, simply to wait for night to come, and to look first at the fading light of twilight, and later to look at the darkness, without talking to

myself, making my head go blank so that no image
would wake me up and trouble me; my eyes half-open
to close the pathways to my nerves and, looking away,
to die temporarily in order to rest. I knew that as soon
as I let my guard down, as soon as I uttered something
in my heart, I would go and stand up, open the notebook, and write down for eight hours straight all the
hatred and frustration that a twenty-year-old boy can
accumulate against the world, filling the pages with
that weeping swill, to wake on that beach dirty and
imbecilic, dead tired, knowing for certain that man
is farther away from all that, and thereby unaware of
the world, disintegrating the mysterious emotion that
unites and jumbles everything up. When everything
was dark, except the starry sky, and the white strip of
foam on the shore sprouting from the retreating sea,
I could no longer keep my eyes open, and no longer
control my fever. My head began to spin; my body
felt weak and sweaty, and I slid between the blankets
half-asleep. Despite my fever, I managed to sleep for
a couple of hours without a single image, without any
nightmares getting in the way.

What woke me suddenly were voices. I lay still
on top of the bed, fixating on the sound. I kept my
eyes wide open and tried to see into the room. It was

a clear night and everything seemed calm. I sat up
a little to look out the window, but when I was about
to look through the frame, I fell backward, shivering.
The voices were no longer audible and it occurred
to me that they might have been in my imagination.
After all, I'd come down with a first-class sunstroke, so
what would be so strange about hearing nonexistent
noises. I stayed in bed, my hands clutching the edges,
ready to jump out if I saw someone come in, throw
myself on him, or flee through the window and run
the two kilometers to the road.

"Lazy bums," I thought. "Miners laid off from
Chuquicamata, or from the saltpeter works themselves, what other people could it be, who would pass
through here, miles from the nearest inhabited area,
at midnight?"

Turning over in bed, I dismissed all my assump-
tions and pulled the covers up to my ears. I tried to go
back to sleep. If what I wanted was to be alone, I told
myself, I had to endure the anxiety and learn not to
fear the night, to live in darkness and enjoy its opaque
sap, just as I was warmly nourished by every day.

The silence calmed me. My head under the quilt,
I remained focused on the night sounds, the movement of the sea, and occasionally, very far off, only

perceptible to those who were attentive, the horns
of the trucks returning from Chuquicamata taking
advantage of the night's cool air. I placed one hand
between my legs and bent my knees, leaned my back
forward, and very slowly whispered a jazz tune. From
time to time, always alert to any external noises, I
would interrupt the song, and although I didn't remember many of the lyrics, I'd start again, making
up the words I needed to finish the melodic phrases. I
don't know if it was sad, one of those Chet Baker songs,
or if the fever produced it, or if the most illusionary
story was beginning to collapse quietly inside me, but
what was certain was that the tears were pouring down
my face, concentrating the fever in my corneas, they
kept flowing and I didn't raise my hand to wipe them
away, but kept allowing them to slip down my chin
and slide down my neck. As I breathed in, deeply, as
if sighing, the air penetrated me more coldly, and I felt
it convulse inside my gut. They weren't the noises I'd
heard before. Nor was the darkness the same. Nor the
absolute silence there was then, silence except for my
broken song, which I kept intoning as if that melody
were protecting me, cradling me warmly, warming the
thoughts that were troubling me.

Everything that was there, curled up, folded in
on itself, boiling at forty degrees Celsius under the
luminous night, all that vain shivering filth, that,
with a gesture of pride and arrogance, I called "I,"
inflating the word, repeating it as I jumped on the dirt
until my cheeks came undone, all the blue wonder, the
blue testimony, the restrained love, the smile, all the
prose and boastfulness, there they were, clinging to
my entrails like the crab that would provide me with
a good breakfast, inert, feeding on my fear, on the
udders of that heavy old cow I had suddenly become,
without agility or grace, in pain every time I stretched
a muscle, and, more afraid, every creak of the cot,
every wind slap against the papers in the room, all
of it separated me more from the rest of the world,
delivered me deep into the mysterious, only it wasn't a
benign mystery, because what it most resembled was a
slow illness, morbid, tasting of the being I was devouring, possessing him standing on the bed, and from
inside, and in the air with a taste of salt, and from
what was not there yet, and from Sunday afternoons
in the province watching the dust on the deserted sidewalks when that taste already appeared in the sweat
under the collar of my white shirt.

For a second I shook my head vigorously, spat on my fingers, and ran them, wet, over my eyelids to cool them, trying again to stay still so that there would be no image that would bring me back to my fear. I listened. There were indeed no noises.

But suddenly, unmistakably, distinctly, someone laughed, a hoarse, low rumbling sound, and this was followed by another, faint, almost feminine laugh. I guessed where they were coming from. They seemed to be on the right side of the car, probably leaning against the wall facing the hill. I lay there in a state of tension. The laughter broke out again, fainter now, like a final comment responding to the earlier laughter. Then a longer silence followed. There was a noise at the back window near the kitchen that made me sit up in bed and squint at the far end of the structure. Then one leg appeared, hung there for a moment, and soon the other one appeared, while the rest of the body made an effort to enter, propelled by the two arms that were gripping the upper part of the window frame. I fumbled for the revolver, which was under the bedspread that had fallen on the floor where I had thrown my pants before going to bed. I reached into my pocket and was relieved to feel the cold metal of the gun. I changed it to my right hand, and, raising

it to eye level, I pointed it at the legs of the man who
was now standing at the window signaling someone
to come closer, and at the same time moving his head
around as if to make sure that no one was watching
him. He even looked in my direction, but, unaccus-
tomed to the darkness of the car, and because the only
thing I was moving was my arm, raising the revolver,
he didn't see me. Before pulling the trigger, I made
a gesture like someone who stops for a moment to
contemplate what he's about to do. A movement like a
quick breath that suddenly serenaded me, that cooled
me down, that took away my fever, as if I had suddenly vomited it out.

"I'm two sandwiches short of a picnic," I thought.
"Absolutely nuts."

I lowered the gun, and just as the other began to
squeeze through the window, I let out a short, shrill
scream as I stood up firmly on my bare feet.

"Who's there!" I shouted, backing away. I instinctively raised the gun.

The one who was climbing in climbed back out
noisily, dropping to the sand in response to a signal
the one who was inside made with his right hand.

Wrinkling my forehead, I tried to get a better look
at what the man was doing in that dark area along the

wall. First, always with my weapon raised, I endured the silence, with something that wasn't exactly patience, but then, the fact that he didn't move, that I didn't even hear him breathe, agitated me, and as I advanced a little I spoke to him.

"What are you doing here?" I asked. "What do you want?" The silence was perfect.

"What are you doing?" I repeated. "I'm armed and I'm aiming at you. I can see you perfectly."

I could feel the revolver wet with perspiration from my hand. I ran my index finger along the trigger to rub it dry.

"Well," I added, violating the tone of false serenity I had used until then, "I'm not going to wait all night for you to answer. If you don't answer, I shoot, understand? I'm armed; you can see that, can't you?"

Before I finished speaking, I saw the mass move, break its stillness with a sort of short jump, which seemed to come in my direction, and throwing myself to one side I pulled the trigger twice, the revolver recoiling and sitting me back on the bed. The vibration I had felt that morning was once again in the air. The flashes of light blinded me momentarily, and as I stood up, I thought I saw the man standing by the window.

"Don't shoot," he said. "Please." I ran my hand across my forehead.

"Are you okay? Did I hurt you?"

"It doesn't seem like it," he said with a lisp.

"I wasn't aiming at your body," I boasted, in case something else might happen.

"Thank you," he said. "We're honest people. Don't worry, boss."

"Tell your friend to come in here," I ordered. He whistled at him through the window.

"He's my son. He's just a boy." I looked outside.

"Pedro, come in here. The young gentleman thought we were thieves, that's why he fired at us. Don't be scared. Just come in."

I set the revolver down and lit a candle. As I rolled the flame so that some wax would spill out and I could secure the candle to the table, I studied the man's features, his massive body, his three-day beard, his green jumpsuit, and then, when he came in, the small one, clad in a worn leather jacket and a pair of shorts.

I found a couple of aspirin on the table, put them in my mouth, and began to suck on them noisily.

"Well. What do you want?" I asked.

The two looked at each other.

"We're just passing through, boss. Going to Antofagasta," the man said. "We didn't think anyone was
here, that's why we tried to get in."

"We were tired," the boy said, running the back of
his hand over his eyes. "We wanted a place to sleep."

"A bed, right, Pedro?"

"Yeah."

"We knew there were beds in these shacks. We'd
been told that. Isn't that right, Pedro?"

The boy nodded.

I was already ashamed as hell at this point.

"Lie down over there," I said, pointing at the two
beds in another compartment.

I went over to them and picked up a demijohn.

"Here's some wine if you're thirsty."

"Don't trouble yourself, boss."

I handed them my bag of supplies and told them to
get something to eat.

"That surprise," I told them, "gave me a headache.
Good night."

"Good night. Thank you. Why'd you go to the
trouble, boss? We're gonna keep quiet over here.
There, Pedro, lie down now."

I went back to bed, reassured, embarrassed,
and before lying down I took out the box with the

ammunition and placed it on the floor within hand's reach. Lying on the bed, playing with the unloaded revolver, spinning it in my right hand, I thought about the world and its people; I thought of all those who live in cities and those who go from one city to another, from one country to another, from one planet to another planet, as if somewhere else things would be better, as if somewhere one could take off one's shoes and, without being afraid of anything anymore, steady in one's own fate, holding it inside one's fist, feeling the courage and gallantry directly in hope's hot beats, say I'm going to stay here and nothing will move me; and I need nothing to be here; and I'm afraid of no one and I can't stop loving anyone, and I can be free to despise whomever I please; and there will be plenty here; and much will be learned by looking at the sea. And this time, stretched out on the bed, I picked up the ammunition one bullet at a time and placed it in the gun's oval magazines, until it was fully loaded. I set the gun down on the floor, and, turning my face to the wall, I closed my eyes and was soon asleep.

When I woke up I looked out the window and there was nothing out there but a bright, warm day. It seemed to be ten o'clock in the morning or thereabouts. I jumped to my feet, and once I was dressed, I went to the other compartment to see my guests. The beds were unmade but there was no trace of either one of them. I grabbed the revolver and the box of ammunition. I went outside, stepped onto the hot sand, and, raising my hands like a sunshade, I looked for them along the length of the beach. I spotted them near a cluster of rocks, making strange contortions on the sand, as if they were burrowing into it with their feet. As I got closer I saw that they were picking something up and throwing it into a wooden box. I also noticed the demijohn of wine and a bucket next to the box. They waved jubilantly when they saw me approaching. When I was close to them, the man moved toward me, holding out a kind of pulsating shellfish.

"Help yourself," he said. "They're clams." I picked it up and chewed it, mindful of its flavor.

"Show me how to dig them up," I said.

"They're buried in the wet sand. Move your foot around and you'll find them."

So I did, and it didn't take me long to find one, which smelled delicious.

We dug for a long time, and when we had filled the box we sat down on the rocks, poured lemon on them, which my guests had brought, and began to eat them, and, in between the digging, we drank a few glasses of wine, first short and refreshing sips, and then long and somniferous ones, until the three of us were half-drunk, and continuously thirsty, and we sent Pedro to fetch another demijohn from the house, and when he came back we drank that one too and went on digging around in the sand and eating clams, until I thought I was going to explode.

I leaned against a rock and closed my eyes while the world pirouetted like a madman and the sea looked red or orange, or almost yellow. I opened them and discovered that my two companions were sleeping, covered with the sand they had rolled around in. Then I remembered my headache, but the feeling I possessed was so sweet that I found it hard to imagine that I could have ever suffered from a headache. I picked up the revolver, aimed at the horizon, and fired. I listened to the echo of the bullet for a few seconds and then I pointed at the horizon again and pulled the trigger, and then I shot the rest of the bullets without stopping to listen to the sound, all the while singing at the top of my lungs one of those instrumental songs they play in cowboy movies.

Then I grabbed the box of ammunition, filled the revolver, and fired at the sky, at the house, breaking two panes of glass, at the wood floating along the shore, at the hills, at a boat that passed in the distance, at everything that I wanted to be dead inside of me. When I had run out of ammunition, and the trigger had missed a click, and I felt my hand burning and sick to my stomach, I got up, shook my two companions without managing to wake them, headed for the house, undressing as I walked, until I encountered the bed, and, smiling, I let myself fall onto it to wait for night to come, free of all restraints, naked as the birds, falling into sleep, sinking into a sweet abyss, thinking, as I lost consciousness of everything around me, about the story I was going to write that night.

public relations

He saw me that afternoon while I was warming my knees the way people from Corrientes do, and he came up to me swinging the paraffin canister.

"You're the Chilean, right?"

I tried to look casual and brushed the edge of the gutter with my bare foot. I used to carry a shoe in my hand in case there was a need to quickly bust someone's head. Unless he was carrying a gun or something, there was little that could happen to me; I'd tasted a knife before and knew what stones felt like; there was nothing left to do but snort through my nostrils and *cccct* out the side of my mouth. A little of that summer sun brightness with hints of rain, a little of that humidity that bogged the birds down in the air, my eyes gave the illusion of looking disdainful.

"You're the Chilean, aren't you?"

He knew I was the Chilean, and I knew he was Miguel. He asked me twice just to give me time to see him scratching his belly, so he could drill my ear with the rhythm he was beating on his drum. "All right," I said to myself, "I'll be thoroughly butchered and then my father will come around and gather up my pieces, tipped off by some neighbor."

"Yes," I answered without looking at him.

He grabbed the front of my shirt and smeared it with his oil-stained fingers. I tried to shake him off by gently pushing his arm away.

"Leave me alone," I said. "If you do anything to me, I'll tell the fellas from Corrientes to give you a good thrashing, big guy."

It was a short-lived ruse. True, I had become a sort of errand boy for the guys from the provinces who lived in the boardinghouse; they'd give me a few cents, and I'd buy them razor blades after their Saturday siesta, or bring them *El Gráfico*, when it wasn't soccer season and they lay in bed naked and singing until their bodies stank. But I was pretty sure they wouldn't lift a finger against a boy from a good family like this one, even if their fucking mothers dragged them out.

That's what Miguel must have been thinking when he raised his elbow and shook his forearm obscenely.

"This is what I'll do to you and everyone in Corrientes, Chilean."

He let go of my shirt as if the ordinary fabric was staining his tidy oil-decorated hand. Then he brushed his contempt across the backside of his suede pants.

"You busted my brother's head, didn't you?"

I looked around the corner to see if anyone from the gang was peeking out. As deserted as a stadium on a weekday! I regretted having cut afternoon class at Casto Munita because I made a mess of my math homework. I imagined all the boys yawning in Smisart's class with their smocks torn and muddy after the soccer match at recess, and swallowing hard I thought that where they were must have been the best place on the planet. The worst of it was that I had the first date of my life with a girl from Zabala Street that afternoon and all the money I had painstakingly looted from my father's meager coffers, and the money from the little jobs I did for the guys from Corrientes, and the money I had earned from the fruit vendor on the corner, I was carrying all of it around in my pocket. For a second I was about to tell him: okay, I'm the Chilean and I'm the one who split your brother's head open; but do me a favor, rip me apart tomorrow, because today I'm going to see a girl, you know what I mean?

"You're the one who busted Quique's head, aren't you?" I stared at the wall in front of me. How incredibly stupid of you to be caught out here at three o'clock, just when the guys from Corrientes were sound asleep.

"It was a street fight," I said. "It was just bad luck."

"You mean you threw the rock and he put his head in front of it, huh?"

"Listen, Miguel," I said. "We don't have to fight. If you want, let's go and I'll apologize to your brother. I'm getting bored with this duking it out over every little thing."

The other sat on top of the canister and started kicking it lightly, his kicks becoming more pronounced as he spoke. I got nervous and felt around in the gutter to see if there was a piece of iron or something.

"What are you, nuts?" he said. "You want me to take you to the hospital to see Quique? Let everyone know that you're the one who ripped off his eyebrow?"

He spat at my feet. I'd already put the money under my sock just below my toes. Now I pretended I needed to tighten my shoelaces.

"So, let them know," I said. "I'll ask him to forgive me, tell him I didn't mean to and that will be that."

Miguel rubbed his knuckles across his teeth.

"I heard right, Chilean. El Quique didn't give you up because of the kind of man he is. Do you know what would have happened if he had opened his mouth? They kick you out of the country. Both you and your good-for-nothing father, you good-for-nothing scum! They deport you, you get me?"

I gulped.

"Seriously?"

He shook his head and sighed dismissively.

"Where do you want to fight?"

I looked him in the eyes, trying to tell him the whole story, but the kid was determined to have his way.

"Now?"

"What do you want? You expect me to wait to see when you have an opening?"

I stood up and brushed the dust off my pants.

"Where?"

"In the vacant lot."

He started to walk in front of me. I could have seized the opportunity to sneak into the boarding-house and hide in my room. The worst thing was that I still had a little bit of honor left. It hadn't rained for days and every time there was a little wind you got

dust in your eyes. I walked around all summer with
eye sores and long hair. I rubbed my eyes, almost
dazed.

"What's wrong with you? Aren't you coming,
pansy-ass?"

"Wait a second; I think I've I got something in my
eye."

He held out his clenched fist and his jaw jutted
forward.

"You're gonna have this in your eye, you fuck."

I moved my hand away from my eyes and started
walking quickly toward the vacant lot.

"Let's go," I said.

There was that ambushing sun, suety along the
lowest part of the clouds and bringing tears to your
eyes when it invades the ground at three o'clock in
the afternoon. At times the almost listless shade from
the dry trees flashed a stretch of darkness, and you
were trusting, unprepared, and suddenly the sidewalk
with its oil-stained cobblestones and rusty horseshoes
jumped like a river of milk veiling the outline of everything in front of you.

Miguel had come up next to me. Either he was
running or I had slowed down.

"How are we going to do this? Just punching, smacking, slapping, with stones, or whatever comes up?"

"Listen to me, Miguel," I said, stopping. "I don't want to fight you. First, because you're much bigger and stronger, and second, because—"

"Second because you're a coward. Get outta here, kid!..." I moved ahead of him before he could slap me and push me away. We were going around the corner and I could feel Miguel's breath on the back of my neck.

"I'm no coward," I said under my breath. "I can't fight with you because I'm not angry. I don't feel like hitting you...People fight when they're angry."

He kneed me in the back, which sent me staggering a few meters forward, but I didn't fall. Actually, he'd pushed me. It could have been one of those awkward jokes we used to play on our friends in the neighborhood.

I turned around to look at him.

"Are you angry now?"

We were facing the abandoned lot. I thought about it for a second and smiled.

"No, Miguel, I'm not. I'm not angry."

Miguel frowned and ran his bewildered hand across his cheek. After a minute, during which I was digging around in the pocket of my overalls, the one over my right thigh, he came over and kicked me in the knee. There was a hollow sound when his shoe hit my knee-cap. By some miracle, there was a hen in the vacant lot and she clucked and cackled all around us. She seemed to be looking for worms. The noises were garbled, except for the one coming from the radio out front, which blasted a comedy show by Aceite Cocinero.

"What about now?"

"What d'you mean, now?"

"Are you angry?"

I put my other hand in my left pocket, and with both I scratched at the cold I felt in my stomach, rubbing hard at the skin there.

"No," I said.

"Are all Chileans as chickenshit as you are, kid?"

"I'm no coward, Miguel. Chileans are brave. There's O'Higgins and José Miguel Carrera and Arturo Prat."

He rummaged in his pockets and pulled out a mangled cigarette butt. He scratched the match across the bottom of his shoe. He inhaled deeply and smoked slowly.

"And we have José de San Martín. Or do you think San Martín was a coward?"

I watched as the smoke dissipated into the gray space above him.

"What the hell do I know!" I said.

"Come on, let's fight."

"Okay," I said, approaching him.

We stood facing each other and his jacket seemed to swell in a sudden burst of sunlight as he stretched out his arms, indicating he was on guard. I imitated him and felt the sweat trickling down my neck. He faked a punch to test me and I didn't move. The guy lowered his arms and, pressing his right fingertips together, he waved them in front of my face.

"Tell me one thing, Chilean. If I hit you, will you defend yourself?"

I blinked for a second, thinking about it.

"Yes, let's get on with it."

"Are you angry?"

"No. Are you?"

"No more than usual," he said. "Let's go."

We brought our elbows up and forward and went around in a semicircle, studying each other. Like a sword-slash, his slap landed flush on my ear. I stepped sideways, and, as I fell, he straightened me up with a left to the ribs. I was still on my feet, but wobbling. I spread my hand across my mouth and although I didn't have time to look, I knew there was blood.

"Are you angry now?"

"A little," I responded. "You gave me a bloody nose, you son of a bitch."

Then he kicked me in the shins and spit in his hand and smacked my ear with it. He shoved me dismissively, though forcefully, and I rolled onto the dust, bruising my cheek. I noticed that there was a boy standing along the side of the vacant lot, staring at me, open-mouthed. Miguel lifted me up by the shirt and pushed me back down again, though he didn't hit me very hard, making me roll on the ground. I could feel my face getting hot and it felt like a fire was burning between my ears. A spurt of piss had leaked out of me and was soaking one of my thighs disgustingly. I stood up and backed away.

"Are you angry, Chilean?"

I wiped the blood off with my wrist.

"I'm going to kill you, you son of a bitch," I said.

Miguel unzipped his leather jacket.

"You poor thing!"

The last thing I saw after those words was his body squeezing me so tight that he rubbed his hand

over my face, coming around from behind as if he
were about to fuck someone. I managed to get away
by throwing an elbow that made him loosen his grip.
We became a bundle of crisp kicks, gnarly knuckles,
a bag of sloppy flailing. Rage engorged my throat,
electrified my fingertips, each slap seemed to pen-
etrate me deeper, make my blood spill more abundantly. It made me want to strangle, to shoot a cat, to
drink water until I fell to my knees. When that punch
cracked my nose and the bone sprang up like a rutting
hawk, I had the first revelatory vision of my life: as if
entangled in the draperies of some provincial circus,
drowned in the tulles and ribbons of a minstrel's
suitcase, falling deep into a sort of mechanical stupor,
of colored poison, of glass bursting, of birds splintering
at the doors, my liver trembled like a dying man, I felt
the rough taste of a cousin's belly in my fingernails,
that hard chest revealing those hot breasts, the earth
was like an immense Gulliver, as in the drawings of
some golden book, only that all rivers and seas were
open wounds, torn slingshots, arrows, blood stagnat-
ing or flowing like a tango through my arteries, and
my hands a bent tree, and my mouth a dead bird
and the night a colossal defeat. I was drunk, feverish,
absolutely unconscious tangled around the waist of

Miguel, who was pounding his fists into his targets as if to drive the hurt into my bones, until he butchered my entrails.

"Miguel," I said. "Miguel, goddamnit, you're killing me!"

But I knew I hadn't uttered those words, that I'd lost my language. That I no longer felt pain, that my voice controlled another body, that this one was only a rehearsal of a body, not the definitive one, that it wasn't important, that after this one I would move on to another one, one that I would choose, one that was inaccessible right now. Then I burst out laughing (my soul laughed), then I floated again in that cobalt sea of my hometown (my soul floated), then I saw those wild beasts on fire and they wet my snout with their tongues (it was my body being born).

When I came to Miguel was lying dead beside me and I dropped the stone.

Blood gushed neatly out of his nostrils and ants crawled around it, squirming in his sweat. I rubbed my ears and leaned against the brick wall, its texture cooling me. I occupied just that one patch of shadow and the rest of the earth was tearing apart like a scream in the pale sun. Maybe the boys would be back from class, maybe they would be smearing butter on their croissants and dipping them in their café con leche; their smocks would be thrown on the bed and they'd be chewing their bread while reading the comics; my father would be riding the subway home with *La Razón* tucked under his arm; the guys from Corrientes would already be practicing the *zamba* with their out-of-tune guitars.

I put my mouth close to his ear and gently lifted one of his eyelids.

"Miguel," I said, "are you dead?"

I grabbed his hands and shook him furiously.

"Don't die, Miguel. Don't be a pussy, *maricon*. Get up...let's go see a doctor."

Then I remembered the boy watching the fight from the street, and I turned around to look for him. He had crossed the sidewalk and when he noticed that I was looking at him, he took off running. I picked up a rusty tin can from a trash heap and walked over to the ditch to fill it with water. I rushed back to keep all the contents from leaking out of a hole during the trip. I bent down and poured the stuff over his nose, neck, and chest.

"Listen, Miguel," I said. "Do me a favor and wake up. I didn't want to kill you. Wake up, Miguel. Think about what your mom's gonna say."

I stood there for a long stretch listening to the screeching trains on Belgrano R. When they didn't slow down I knew it was the expresses. I counted five trains before running back to the irrigation ditch and returning with another can of water. While I was drenching him with water again, it occurred to me to go and look for a guy from Santiago del Estero I knew who was a porter in the fruit store. Once I'd injured my knee in a soccer match and he had patched it up with a bandage and everything. He said he was going to study medicine, but in the meantime he had taken a first-aid course.

"Hey, Miguel, wake up a little bit at least. I'm going to take you to Negro's to get your nose fixed. Don't be such a sleepyhead. El Negro is going to make your nose as good as new if you're still alive."

I turned him over and poured the rest of the liquid over his neck. I thought I heard him moan and that reminded me of a Yon Uein movie where John Wayne's character put his ear to the heart of a guy who was shot and everything, not like this one who had a simple bump on his head, and he said he was still alive, because he could still hear that noise like a snare drum. I turned him over again and the ticking sound was clearly audible.

"I've already noticed that you're not dead, Miguel. Now it's just a matter of you waking up so that I can take you to el Negro. If I drag you along like this, people will think I murdered you, understand?"

The worst part of it all was that a few abrupt drops had started to fall and the sky became wet and filthy all over, and there was nowhere to put Miguel so that he wouldn't get drenched. There was a small roof jutting out on one side, but it would barely protect someone who could stand up. Then it occurred to me that the best thing I could do was to let the rain soak Miguel, saving me from going to the ditch every now and then to fetch water with that moldy, leaky can. I rummaged through the guy's pockets and came across another cigarette that was even more mangled than the first one and walked to the outcropping, hoping the rain would subside. For a few minutes there was a little preliminary thunder and lightning and a minor excuse for rain of pure crap quality that didn't wet anything. The cigarette smoke felt nice and warm as it crept down my neck, and I amused myself by blowing circles, while the ground began to become softly boggy, and the thunder left the crackle to the side of the Barrancas. But when the downpour broke loose like a frightened dog, the puddles started to get deep and I walked over to Miguel in case his face was in a puddle that was going to drown him. It was getting dark everywhere around us, even though it was early, and the mire plunked, sucked my foot in up to my ankles three times before I reached him. I was happy to find him with his eyes open and his head in a more or less dry spot.

"What happened?" he said, starting to stand up, supporting himself with his palms.

I picked up a newspaper to cover my head.

"We had a fight," I replied.

He sat down in the mud and zipped up his jacket, closing it around his neck.

"Yes, I know that. But what happened to me?"

"I don't know. I busted your nose and thought you'd died."

He shook his head, bewildered, and grabbed the hand I was offering to pull him up.

"You beat me, then," he said. "You knocked me out cold."

I could barely see his face through all that water. He rested his little finger on the disaster and carefully pushed it back into his nose. Then he tilted his head and slapped his upper ear with his palm as if he wanted to knock something out of there. As if he wanted to clear away the mess that was in there, I guess.

"It's raining," he said.

I picked up a newspaper and held it out to him.

"You know what? Probably best we stop fighting, Chilean. We could catch a cold."

"Okay," I said.

We walked, jumping across the puddles, and took shelter in a small entryway. As we were wringing out our pants, I wiggled my toes to see if the money was still there. I also noticed that my cheek was swollen. I dribbled a little spit on the back of my hand and wiped it over it to calm the heat.

"You broke my jaw," I told him.

He cupped my jaw in his hand and examined it for a moment.

"Then we're even," he ruled. I nodded gravely.

"Hey, Miguel... Let me buy you an ice cream."

"You got dough?"

I took off my shoe and, pulling off my sock, showed him the cash.

"Let's go."

The rain stopped as we were walking to the station and we shifted from walking along the buildings and walls to the street, so we could kick the cans that came out in the middle of O'Higgins Avenue. When we finally got to Barrancas I bought two *marron glacé* cones.

We licked the ice cream without looking at each other and when I was about to finish with my cone, I told him:

"Look, Miguel. When you smashed my jaw and cracked my ribs I had a kind of vision."

"What are you talking about?"

"I was stunned and saw the moment I was born. I could feel my mother run her tongue along my cheek. Only my parents were like flames, you know what I mean?"

Miguel nibbled a crumb dangling from his fingernail and then put his hands in his pockets.

"What happened to you is that you had a hallucination, do you know what that is?"

"No," I said.

"I don't really know either. But a hallucination is like a premonition of something, you know what I mean?"

"Yes," I murmured.

But I didn't understand.

I counted the money I still had and realized that life wasn't really short or long. That there would always be just enough time.

"Would you eat some pizza?"

"Okay."

It was raining again outside the ice cream parlor and the pizza was soft and the cheese and tomato were tangled in abundant flaccid gushes across the dough.

Three months later in some Belgrano entryway I made love to a girl for the first time in my life. I didn't care that I had spent all my money that afternoon, or that I hadn't gone to see the girl on Zabala Street. The money I spent I filed under public relations.

among all things,
the first is the sea

"Among all things, the first is the sea," my cousin said. "And then the sun, and then the night. If that's what you wanted to know, you're all set. Toss me the hammer."

I found the tool under the car's mud flaps and I quickly handed it to him. He took it and started to beat on a pipe with short, violent whacks; it was probably the exhaust pipe; I don't know anything about cars.

"It needs to be straightened," he said as he banged on it.

"That's not what I wanted to know," I replied.

"What *didn't* you want to know?"

"Well...the thing about the sea, and then the sun, and then the wind," I said.

"Not the wind. After the sun, night."

"Right. Well, it wasn't that."

"Okay," my cousin said.

"You studied literature."

"Right. And..."

"You used to be Angelica's boyfriend," I added.

"What'd you say?"

"You can't hear me if you're banging on that pipe the whole time," I yelled.

As he continued to beat the pipe, he turned around for a second and looked at me. Then he looked at the pipe again, turned it over, and started to hit it on the other side.

"You're not being very polite," I said. "Your manners annoy me."

"So I guess what you're saying is that you don't think the sea comes first, right?"

"I don't have anything to say about that."

"Have you talked to my father?"

"Yes."

"I can understand that he's worried. He doesn't know."

"Neither do I."

He stopped hammering, looked at the sky, and blinked. He glanced at the car, walked around it, and grabbed me by the shoulder and we walked over to the grass and sat in silence.

"You're the best one in the family, the best one out of all of us," he told me.

"No way!" I said.

"I'm serious. You're going to be somebody."

"Enough with that," I said. "You're going to be somebody, too. The truth is, everyone's someone in one way or another."

"Not yet," he said.

"Your dad worries about you," I commented.

"I don't like the sound of that."

"He wants you to finish your studies. And I think he's right if you want to know what I think."

He jumped to his feet. He went inside, entering through the back of the kitchen. After a moment he pushed the door open with one foot and came out with two soft drinks in his hands. He sat down next to me and handed me one.

"What was it you were saying?" he said.

"Your dad worries about you."

"No. Before that."

"That you used to be Angelica's boyfriend," I said.

"For cryin' out loud!"

"I liked that she was your girlfriend."

"Then we'll pick her up when I'm done with the car."

"Are you thinking of bringing her with us?"

"I promised her I would," he said. Then he added: "University...it's not for me. A guy like me has no business being in college."

He leaned back against the apple tree.

"So what do you want to do?" I asked. "You have some money, good grades; you had Angelica. What do you really want?"

He stretched out his arms, scrunched up his face, and then shrugged his shoulders.

"To understand," he said.

"Understand what?" I insisted.

"Everything. I'm really stupid."

"You're the smartest one in the family," I said. "You're no fool. Why would you stop studying? No one's ever had better grades than you. What's wrong with you?"

He finished his soda. He rolled the bottle across the grass; it rolled until it hit my shoe.

"Let's get this car wrapped up," he said. "Otherwise we're not going to have any sun when we get to the beach."

Yet, he continued leaning against the tree and didn't seem to have any apparent intention of moving on with the work. I got up and put some tools in the toolbox.

"Sometimes things just happen," he said.

"Like what?" I said.

"I don't know. Things," he said.

"I don't know what you're talking about," I replied. "Let's finish this up."

He walked to the car, opened the door, and started the engine. Then he leaned over the steering wheel, his eyes lost on something in the distance, and ran his hand across the windshield.

"I like to feel like I'm free," he said. "To feel my hands at work, to touch my naked body, to have a conversation. I'd like my wife to be independent. I'd like to have the freedom to fuck my wife when we want and have a conversation. Do you know what I mean?"

"You should be a writer," I said.

"That's what I'm going to do."

Then he leaned back and snorted loudly.

"The best," he said. "These things happen to people. Do you think I'm being dramatic?"

"Yes," I said.

"Does that bother you?"

"No," I answered. "I know who you are."

"Out of all of us in this family, you're the best one," he said. "And you didn't even go to college."

"College isn't for me."

He reached out his hand, wrinkled up his face, and pointed a finger at his chest.

"Me neither."

"But with you, yes," I affirmed.

"Maybe you're right," he replied. "You know, these things happen."

"So what am I supposed to tell your father now?"

"Don't tell him anything. Go get our swimsuits and let's go."

"Let's finish up the car."

"It's good to go," he replied. "I'll attach the muffler and we'll leave."

I turned around and as I was pushing the front door of the house open, he whistled for me to stop.

"This motherfucking car had been broken down, *en panne*, for three months."

He looked at me, then raised his eyebrows, and raised his head in a kind of query.

"Okay?" he asked.

"Okay," I said. "And do you want to know something else?"

"Shoot," he said.

"If you're going to write, you're going to be the best writer there is. You want to know why?" I said as I opened the door.

"Shoot."

"Because you never brag about anything."

"Right. But that's not enough. In college we study writers who brag all the time."

"That's different. You want to understand."

"That's not enough either. I'm not pedantic."

"Okay," I said. "What the hell, you're dramatic!"

"Good," he said. "Out of all of us in this family, you're the best one. Go get the bathing suits."

I went inside and ran up the stairs; I grabbed the bathing suits from my cousin's room, two towels, a pack of cigarettes, and threw them into my bag. When I was about to go downstairs, I bumped into my uncle, who was coming out of his room.

"What's he have to say?" he asked. "What's he doing now?"

"He fixed the car. We're going to the beach."

"So he fixed the car, you say. He's definitely a smart kid. And what's he say about going back to college?"

"Nothing," I answered.

"Nothing?" he said.

"Don't worry. We have to get going."

"I have to worry. He's my son."

"He'll keep studying," I said. "And if you really want to know, he can't survive without studying."

"How do you know?"

"Sometimes these things happen," I replied. And I ran down the stairs.

Once we were settled inside the car, we took off at full speed. The car was manageable, and although it had never sounded so smooth, my cousin didn't brag about it. After a little while, and right at noon, we stopped in front of Angelica's house and my cousin went inside to get her. I too got out of the car, and I walked into the corner diner, picked up the phone, and notified the office that I wouldn't be going to work that afternoon because I was sick. Then I ordered a soft drink, put a coin in the slot machine, and lit a cigarette.

When I got back to the car I noticed that my cousin's expression had changed. His mouth was twisted into a grimace and he was frowning. Angelica, seated next to him, greeted me with a faint smile and I sat on her left side, bent my elbow on the open window, and kept my mouth shut. After a while, we turned onto the coastal highway, and later we passed by Los Cerrillos, and then through Melipilla. My cousin was driving at full speed and hadn't said a word. Angelica and I simply looked at the scenery and smoked cigarettes.

When we got to Cartagena, he slowed down and we cruised along the waterfront, looking at the people, the hills, and the sea. Then he picked up speed again and we didn't stop until we reached Las Cruces.

"We'll stop here," he said. "Do you like it?"

"A lot," I answered. "I thought you'd gone mute."

"And you?" he asked Angelica.

"It's all right."

We undressed in the car, put on our swimsuits, and walked slowly across the sand to lie down near the water's edge.

My cousin buried his face into the sand, stretched out his arms, and started playing around, picking up fistfuls of sand, squeezing them, and then slowly releasing them. Angelica lay on her back and I sat there, smoking and thinking about her tan, her black hair shining on the sand, and desiring her. That's how I'd met her the year before, when my cousin brought me along that summer and introduced me to her, and told me that she was "the one," and that she was a little flighty, but that she was "the one" all the same.

Now she had changed, my cousin had been changing her, without forcing anything, imperceptibly, making her into a world, molding her, filling her with life, filling her youthful world with his strength.

"What's wrong with him?" I said.

"He got that way," she replied. "Suddenly."

"What do you mean?" I asked.

"I don't know. What does he want? I've been okay," she said. "What does he want?"

"To understand."

She sat up and flipped a cigarette out of the pack and I lit it for her.

"I'll never really know who he is. He's different," she said.

"Yes," I replied. "He's different."

"What do you think?"

"That everything winds up getting worked out. What do you want me to think?" I turned around and lay down with my back to the sun.

"I hope so," she said.

"Don't worry."

Later my cousin got up and with a simple gesture took Angelica to the sea. Almost as soon as they reached the water, they stopped and chatted for a few minutes. Then they waded into the sea and swam for a while. I lit a cigarette and smoked it calmly, looking at the sky with my eyes turned toward the sun. The day was clear, there was no wind, and only a few birds fluttered high above.

Angelica came running up to me, dried her face and legs, sat on the towel, adjusted her hair, and smiled.

"Everything's fine," she said.

"Good," I said. "What's he doing now?"

"He's floating. He likes to lie on his back and float."

"He's going to be a writer," I said.

We continued to chat for over an hour and my cousin kept floating, and swimming, and sometimes he'd dive off a rock. Then I went into the water, swam up to him, and we had a race, which I won. We sat on a rock, and my cousin panted and burst out laughing.

"Wait until I read you some poems I made up out of the blue."

"All right," I said. "Let's wait until it gets dark."

"That's a good idea," he said.

As we drove back, Angelica and my cousin sat in the back and I drove to Santiago with the windows down and the warm November wind blowing violently against my face. We dropped Angelica off and once we got home we went into the kitchen, put some cheese on some *marraquetas*, and sank our teeth into them. Later we went up to his room. My cousin sat down at his desk, took out two books and a few sheets of paper.

"The sea was beautiful," he said.

"It sure was."

"For me it's the first thing, the most important," he added. Then he handed me one of the books.

"Latin."

Then he handed me the other one.

"Classic Spanish literature, Cervantes."

"Lope de Vega," I said.

"The Archpriest of Hita," he said.

"*Life is a dream*," I said.

"Fantastic books," he said. "Great writers, yes, sir!"

Then he turned the chair around, leaned his elbows on the desk, rested his head on his hands, and started to read. I opened *Don Quixote* to chapter thirty-three, stretched back on the bed, and read until three in the morning. Then I put the book on the floor and covered my face with my pillow, and before long I fell asleep. As far as I remember, my cousin was still studying.

the cyclist from
san cristóbal

... and so downcast did I become,
that I rose high, so high,
that I hunted down the hunt itself...

ST. JOHN OF THE CROSS

B esides, it was my birthday. I saw that Russian Sputnik that the newspapers talked so much about from the Alameda balcony, and it was crossing the sky parsimoniously and I didn't even drink that much because the next day we had the first qualifying trials of the season and my mother was sick in a room no bigger than a closet. I had no choice but to pedal with my legs in the air and the back of my neck against the floor tiles so that my muscles would firm up, and I could stomp on the pedals in the morning with that style of mine which was the subject of an article in *Estadio*. While Mamá was in a feverish levitation, I began to wander the hallways devouring, crumb by crumb, the cakes that Aunt Margarita had given me, meticulously picking apart the pieces of candied fruit with the tip of my tongue and spitting them out the side, which was a totally disgusting thing to do. My old man would step out every so often to taste the punch, but each time he would take five minutes to stir it, and he would sigh, and then he would pick at the peaches that floated like castaways in the mixture of cheap white wine, and pisco, and orange, and soda.

We both needed something that would make the night pass more quickly and bring the morning more urgently. I made up my mind to stop exercising and polish my shoes; the old man was flipping through the directory with the likely idea of calling an ambulance, and the sky was clear, and the night was very warm, and Mamá was talking in her sleep: "I'm burning up," not so softly that we couldn't hear what she was saying through the open door.

But that was a rough night filled with fear, a bitch that didn't relax one bit. Looking up at the stars was the same as counting cacti in a desert, like biting your

cuticles to the point of bleeding, like reading a Dostoyevsky novel. Then Papá would come into the room
and repeat the same implausible arguments in my
mother's ear, that the injection would lower her fever,
that the sun had already come up, that the doctor was
going to come early in the morning before heading to
Cartagena to go fishing.

In the end, we tricked her with the dark. We made
use of that milky thing the sky has when it's late and
we wanted to make her think it was dawn (if I'd been
pushed a little I could have made out a rooster crow-
ing in the middle of it all).

It could have been any time between three and
four o'clock when I went into the kitchen to make
breakfast. As if they were working in tandem, the
whistling of the kettle and my mother's screams grew
louder and louder. Papá appeared in the doorway.

"I can't bring myself to go in," he said.

He was pale and fat and his shirt was simply dripping. We could hear Mamá saying: "Get the doctor."

"He said he'd stop by first thing in the morning,"
my old man repeated for the fifth time.

I had been mesmerized by the lid bouncing over
the kicking steam.

"She's going to die," I said.

Papá began to pat the pockets all over his body. A
sign that he wanted to smoke. Now he'd have a hell of
a time finding the cigarettes and then the same thing
would happen with the matches and then I'd have to
light it for him from the gas stove.

"You think so?"

I raised my eyebrows as high as I could and sighed.

"Give it here and I'll light your cigarette."

As I was getting closer to the flame, I was a little
confused that the fire wasn't hurting my nose like all
the other times. I handed the cigarette to my father,
without turning my head, and consciously placed my
little finger on the small bundle of fire. It was as if I
hadn't. I thought, "This finger died or something,"
but you couldn't think of the death of a finger without
laughing a little, so I stretched out my whole palm and
this time I touched my fingertips to the gas tubing,
each one of the little holes, digging at the very roots of
the flames. Papá walked from one end of the hallway to the other, taking care to tip all the ash on his
collar, to coat his whiskers with tobacco dust. I made
the most of the opportunity to take it a little further,
and put my wrists over the flame to toast them a little,
and then my elbows, and then all my fingers again.
I turned off the gas, spit a little saliva on my hands,

which felt dry, and carried the basket of stale bread, the jam jar, and a brand-new package of butter to the dining room.

When Papá sat down at the table I should have started to cry. He twisted his neck, he lowered his eyes to look into the bitter coffee as if that's where the resignation of the planet was concentrated, and then he said something, but I didn't hear him, because he seemed to be holding an incredulous dialogue with something intimate, a kidney for example, or a femur. Then he reached into his open shirt and brushed the tangle of hairs that coiled on his chest. There was a basket of plums, apricots, and peaches, which were a little bruised, on the table. For a moment the fruit remained unspoiled and cradled, and I stared at the wall like I was being shown a movie or something. Finally, I grabbed an apricot and rubbed it on my collar until I got a fairly passable shine. My old man, following my lead, picked up a plum.

"My old lady's gonna die," he said.

I rubbed my neck hard. Now I was trying to wrap my head around the fact that I hadn't been burned. I licked the leftovers on the fruit pit with my tongue, and with my hands I began to press the crumbs on the table together, gathering them in little piles, and then

I would use my index finger to kick them between
the cup and the breadbasket. At the same time, I was
pushing the pit against my cheekbone, and I imagined
that I had a major logjam stuck in my back teeth,
making me look serious; I thought I'd discovered the
meaning of why I had become incombustible, if one
can say such a thing. The thing wasn't very clear, but
it had the same evidence that allows for a rain pre-
diction when the southern lapwing is puffing hard in
the air: if Mamá was going to die, I would also have
to emigrate from the planet. The fire thing was like
a synopsis of a scary movie, or maybe it was just my
own blah blahing, and the only thing that happened
was that my visits to the biographer had turned me
into an addict.

I looked at Papá and, just as I was about to
tell him, he pressed his chubby palms together in
front of his eyes until the space between them was
impenetrable.

"She'll live," I said. It's easy to get scared with a
fever.

"It's like the body's defense system."

I cleared my throat.

"If I win the race we'll have some money. We
could get her into a decent clinic."

"If she doesn't die."

I spit the little pit, smooth from so much sucking, over my shoulder. The old man ventured to take a bite out of a peach so juicy it was drinkable. We heard Mamá complaining in her bedroom; this time she didn't use any words. I finished my coffee in three gulps, almost comforted that it burned the roof of my mouth. I slipped a *marraqueta* into my pocket, and when I got up, the crumbs seemed to gather to refresh themselves in a kind of wine cup, which looked fresh, though the stains on the tablecloth had been there for as long as Mamá had been in bed, for a month at least.

I used a casual tone to say goodbye, a little bit like a gringo, we might say.

"I'm taking off."

In response to this, Papá twisted his neck and turned back to the night.

"What time's the race?" he asked, sipping his coffee.

I felt like a pig, and not exactly one of those likable fools in the comics.

"Nine o'clock. I'm going to do a little warm-up first."

I took the pant clips out of my pocket and tugged the bag with my gear in it over my shoulder. I was

humming a Beatles song at the same time, one of
those psychedelic ones.

"It might do you some good to get some sleep,"
Papá suggested. "It's been two nights since..."

"I feel fine," I said, moving toward the door.

"Okay then."

"Your coffee's going to get cold."

I closed the door as sweetly as I could, as if I were
making out with a girl, and then I loosened the lock
on my bike, unfastening it from the bars on the stair
railing. I tucked it under my arm, and without waiting
for the elevator I ran down the four flights of stairs
to the street. I stood there for a minute caressing and
turning the tires, not knowing where to start, while
now the early morning air was blowing, a little cold, a
little slow.

I got on, and with a single pedal push I glided
down the side of the road and went along the Alameda to Plaza Bulnes, and I curved through the
roundabout to the fountain in the plaza, and immediately turned left to Negro Tobar's boîte and crouched
under the awning to listen to the music coming out of
the basement. What really annoyed me was not being
able to smoke, not being able to shatter that image
of the perfect athlete that our coach had drilled into

the backs of our heads. Whenever I arrived reeking
of tobacco, he would smell my tongue and *get outta
here* he'd say. But on top of everything else, I was like
a foreigner in Santiago's early morning. Maybe I was
the only boy in Santiago whose mother was dying, the
only and absolute numbskull in the galaxy who had
not known how to get a girl to liven up his partyless
Saturday nights, the only and definitive animal who
cried when he was told gloomy stories. And suddenly
I located the theme of the quartet, and to be exact it
was Lucho Aránguiz's trumpet phrasing "I can't give
you more than love, baby, that's all I can give you,"
and two silent couples passed in front of the awning,
like ashes that the school tough had scattered across
the sidewalks, and there was something mournful
and unforgettable in the whisper of the corner water
tap, and the milkman's carriage seemed to emerge
from the silver sea above the pool, slow in spite of his
horses' verve, and the wind was carrying cigarette
wrappers and ice-pop wrappers, and the drummer
was dragging the song out like a long string that has
nothing tied to its end—*shashá-dá-dá*—and a drunk
young man came out of the basement to wipe his
sweaty nose, his eyes skating here and there, red with
smoke, the knot of his tie dislocated, his hair gathered

around his temples, and the orchestra played the
tango, *sophisticated-like*, always the same, someone is
always looking hopeful, and the buildings on Bulnes
Avenue at any moment could fall down dead, and
then the wind would blow even more disjointedly, it
would make ships weathercocks, barges and masts of
the scaffolding, it would make alcohol barrels of modern heaters, it would transform doors into seagulls,
parquets into foam, radios and irons into fish, lovers'
beds would catch fire, formal suits and gowns, underpants, bracelets would be crabs, and they would be
mollusks, and they would be grit, and to each face the
hurricane would give its own face, a mask to the old
man, fits of laughter to the student, to the young virgin the sweetest pollen, all toppled over by the clouds,
all crashing against the planets, hollowed out in death,
and me among them pedaling through the hurricane
with my bicycle saying don't die Mamá, singing *Lucy
in the sky with diamonds*, and the useless policemen
with their riding crops whipping imaginary colts,
astride the wind, whipped by parks as high as kites,
by statues, and me reciting the last verses I learned in
Spanish class, almost reluctantly, drawing something
pornographic in Aguilera's notebook, stealing Koj-
man's field trip provisions, sticking a pencil in Flaco

Leiva's ass, me reciting, and the young man tightened
his belt with the same parsimony that a man thirsty
for tenderness abandons a lover's bed, and suddenly he
sang frivolously, distracted from the lyrics, as if each
song were just a rain shower before the calm, and then
he staggered down the stairs, and Luchito Aránguiz
seized a "one," a solo on the trumpet, and began
to rush it, and everything became jazz, and when I
wanted to look for a bit of the early morning air that
would cool my palate, my throat, the jackrabbit that
was ripping through my belly and my liver, my head
flew against the wall, violent, noisy, and I got dazed,
and I dug into my pants, and pulled out the pack, and
I smoked with relish, with greed, while I was sliding
down the wall until I laid my body against the tiles on
the floor, and then I crossed my palms and I dedicated
myself to sleep.

The drums woke me, the batons and bugles of
some glorious man circling the Santiago Ferris wheel
not on his way to any war, though he did seem to be
decked out as if for a party. It was enough for me to
get on my bike and race around for a couple of blocks
to witness the resurrection of the wafer makers, the
miserable old women, the peanut sellers, the smooth-
faced teenagers in fashionable shirts and boots. If

the San Francisco clock wasn't lying this time, I had only seven minutes left to reach the starting line at San Cristóbal. Although my body was being eaten by cramps, my sneakers on the rubber pedals hadn't lost their accuracy. Otherwise there was sunshine soaring above like this and the sidewalks looked almost deserted.

When I crossed Pío Nono, things started to get lively. I noticed that the other riders lining the hill doing warm-ups were giving me a few sidelong glances. I could see Lopez from Audax wiping his nose, Ferruto from Green pumping up a tire, and the guys from my team listening to our coach's instructions.

When I joined the group, they looked at me reproachfully but didn't get distracted. I took advantage of the situation and behaved like a diva.

"Do I have time to make a phone call?" I said. The coach pointed to the dressing room.

"Go get dressed."

I wheeled my bike to the equipment manager.

"It's urgent," I explained. "I have to call home."

"What for?"

But before I could explain, I pictured myself in the soda fountain across the street, sandwiched between kids who should be in a zoo and sallow-faced drunks, dialing home to ask my father … what? Did the old lady die? Did the doctor come by the house? How's Mamá doing?

"It doesn't matter," I replied. "I'm going to get dressed."

I dove into the tent and devoted my full attention to taking off my clothes. When I had stripped completely I proceeded to claw at my thighs and then my calves and heels until I felt my body responding to me. I painstakingly compressed my belly with the elastic waistband, and then used my wool socks to cover up all the maroon traces my fingernails had left. As I tightened my shorts and pulled the elastic in my T-shirt tighter I knew I was going to win the race. I felt haggard, my throat cracked, a bitter taste on my tongue, my legs stiff as a mule's, and I was going to win the race. I was going to beat the coach, beat Lopez, beat Ferruto, beat my own teammates, beat my father, beat my schoolmates and my teachers, beat my very bones, my head, my belly, my own dissolution, beat my death and that of my mother, beat the president of the Republic, beat Russia and the United States, beat the bees, the fish, the birds, the flower pollen; I was going to win by beating the galaxy.

I grabbed an elastic wrap and double-tightened the instep, sole, and ankle of each of my feet. When I'd tied them together like a tight fist, my ten fleshy, aggressive, flexible toes were all that showed.

I left the tent. "I'm a beast," I thought when the race judge raised his gun, "I'm going to win this race because I have claws and hooves at the end of each foot." I heard the gun and with two sharp, slashing lunges down on the pedals, I took the lead up the first hill. As soon as the slope eased, I let the sun slowly liquefy on the back of my neck. I didn't need to look too far back to spot Pizarnick from team Ferroviario, glued to my ass. I felt sorry for the boy, for his team, for his coach, who would have told him: "If he takes the lead, stick to him for as long as you can, but be calm, use your head, you understand?" because if I wanted to, I could set a pace right there that would have the boy vomiting in less than five minutes, with his lungs churning, failed, incredulous. At the first turn the sun disappeared, and I raised my head to the Virgin of the Hill, and she looked sweetly aloof, incorruptible. I decided to be intelligent, and I let Pizarnick take the lead by slowing the pace of my pedaling abruptly. But the boy was riding with the Bible on his saddle: he slowed when he caught up with me, and a blond-haired boy from the Stade Français passed me hard and took the lead. I cocked my neck to the left and smiled at Pizarnick. "Who's that?" I said. The kid didn't look back at me. "What?" he gasped.

"Who's that?" I repeated. "The one who just passed us." He didn't seem to notice that we were lagging a few meters behind. "I don't know him," he said. "Did you see what kind of bike he had?" "A Legnano," I replied. "What are you thinking about?" But this time he didn't answer me. I realized that he had been thinking the whole time whether now that I had lost the lead he should stick to the new leader or not. If he had only asked me, I would have warned him; too bad his Bible transmitted with only one antenna. A steeper slope, and good night to the vicars. He pushed and pedaled until he got close to the blond kid, and almost desperately looked back, measuring the distance. I looked around for another contender to talk to, but I was only about twenty meters away from the leaders, and the other riders were just showing their noses around the bend. I wrapped my fingers around the clattering in the middle of the handlebars, and with one hand placed in the center I maneuvered the gear levers. How could I be so alone, all of a sudden! Where did the blond and Pizarnick go? And what about González, and the kids from the club, and those from Audax Italiano? Why was I starting to feel short of breath now, why was the space crawling over the rooftops of Santiago, crushing?

Why was my sweat hurting my eyelashes and getting into my eyes, clouding everything? This heart of mine wasn't beating so hard to get blood into my legs, or to make my ears burn, or to make my butt harder in the saddle, and my lunges stronger. This heart of mine was betraying me, it was making me sick to my stomach, it was spurting blood from my nostrils, it was exuding steam into my eyes, it was churning my arteries, it was rotating in my diaphragm, it was leaving me perfectly relinquished to an anchor, to my body made into a rope, to my lack of grace, to my succumbing.

"Pizarnick!" I shouted. "Stop, for fuck's sake, I'm dying!"

But my words rippled between temple and temple, between my upper and lower teeth, between my saliva and carotids. My words were a perfect circle of flesh: I'd never said anything. I'd never spoken to anyone on earth before. I had been a repeating image in the shop windows, in the mirrors, in the winter pools, in the girls' eyes all the time thick with black paint. And maybe now—pedal by pedal, pushing down and pushing down, bursting and bursting—the same silence was coming to Mamá— and I was going up and up and up and down and down and down—asphyxiation's same blue death— strike and strike, turn and turn—the death of dirty noses and liquid sounds in the throat—and I ser- pentine whirlwind bucking gear turning—the white and definitive death—no one was going to bring me down, mother!—and the panting of how many three four five ten cyclists who would pass me, or was it me catching up with the leaders, and for an instant I had my eyes half-open above the abyss and I had to clench my eyelashes tightly so that all Santiago would not float up and drown me, lifting me high, and then I would fall, splintering my head on a cobblestone street, over garbage dumps full of cats, over despica- ble corners. Poisoned, my free hand plunged into my mouth, then biting my wrists, I had a last moment of clarity: a certainty without judgment, untranslat- able, captivating, slowly blissful, that yes, very well, perfectly well, brother, that this end was mine, that my annihilation was mine, that it was enough for me to pedal harder and win this race risking even my death, that even I myself could manage what little body I had left, those throbbing toes on my feet, feverish, concluding, toes angels tentacles hooves, toes claws scalpels, apocalyptic toes, definitive toes, little shit fingers, and push the rudder to either side, east or west, north or south, face and seal, or nothing, or perhaps always remain northsoutheastwest-facestamp, moving immobile, blunt. Then I filled my face with this hand and I slapped my sweat away and I exploded my cowardice; laugh, asshole, I said to myself, laugh, little man, laugh because you are alone at the top, because nobody puts his foot down at that crucial moment like you on the downhill descent.

And from that last surge that came from the soles of my feet filling my thighs and hips and chest and neck and forehead with beautiful, boisterous, hot blood, from a crowning, from my body's assault against God, from an irresistible course, I felt the slope easing for a second and I opened my eyes and looked directly into the sun, and then, yes, the tires were giving off smoke and screeching, the chains sang, the handlebars flew away like a bird's head, sharp against the sky, and the spokes of the wheel shattered the sun into a thousand pieces and threw them all over the place, and then I heard, I heard Oh my God! the people cheering for me on top of vans, the little boys shrieking at the edge of the downhill curve, the loudspeaker announcing the rankings of the first five riders; and while the free fall was coming, wild on the new asphalt, one of the organizers drenched me from head to toe laughing, and twenty meters ahead, I was dripping, laughing, easy, someone looked at me, a colorful girl, and said "wet as a young chicken," and it was time to leave the nonsense behind, the track was slippery, and it was time again to be full-on intelligent, to use the brakes, to dance around the curve like a tango or a waltz in full orchestra.

Now the wind that I was creating (the space was serene and transparent) was churning the dirt up and across my pupils, and I almost broke my neck when I twisted around to see who was second. El Rucio, the blond kid, of course. But unless he had a pact with the devil he wouldn't overtake me in the descent, for a very simple reason the sports magazines explain in great detail but that can be summarized like this: I never used the handbrake; I would only put my shoe on my tires when the curves were cornered. Race after race, I was the only competitive beast in the city on my bike. The metal frame, the wheels, the leather, the saddle, the eyes, the headlight, the handlebars, were one and the same quarrel with my back, my belly, my rigid pile of bones.

I crossed the finish line and got off the bike as I coasted along. I endured the shoulder and back slaps, the hugs from the coach, the photos by the kids from Estadio, and I downed a Coke in one gulp. Then I took my bike and walked along the side of the road toward the apartment.

A hesitation I had in front of the door, a last doubt, perhaps the shadow of an uncertainty, the thought that everything had been a trap, a trick, as if the flashing of the Milky Way, the sun multiplying in the streets, the silence, as if all of it were the synopsis of a movie that would never appear, not in the city center, not with the neighborhood biographers, not in the imagination of any man.

I pressed the buzzer briefly and dramatically, twice, three times. Papá opened the door, as if he had forgotten that he lived in a city where people go from house to house knocking on doors, ringing doorbells, visiting each other.

"Mamá?" I asked.

The old man widened the opening, smiling.

"She's okay." He put his hand on my back and pointed to the bedroom. "Go in and see her."

I cleared my throat, which was a scandalous racket, and turned around in the middle of the hallway.

"What's she doing?"

"She's having lunch."

I walked over to her bed, quietly, fascinated by how elegantly she was placing the spoonfuls of soup between her lips. Her skin was pasty and the wrinkles on her forehead had grown a centimeter deeper, but she spooned with grace, with rhythm, with...hunger.

I sat on the edge of the bed, spellbound.

"How did it go?" she asked, nibbling on a soda cracker.

I gave her a movie-like smile.

"Good, Mamá. Good."

There was an angel hair noodle on her pink shawl. I reached over to remove it. Mamá caught my hand, suspended it in movement, and sweetly kissed my wrist.

"How do you feel, Má?"

She ran her hand down the back of my neck now, and then arranged the strands of hair over my forehead.

"Okay, my little boy. Do your mother a favor, will you?"

I asked her with my eyebrows.

"Go get some salt. This soup isn't very tasty."

I got up, and before heading to the dining room, I poked my head into the kitchen to see my father.

"Did you talk to her? She's upbeat, isn't she?"

I stared at him, scratching my cheek with pleasure.

"Do you know what she wants, Papá? Do you know what she sent me to get?"

My old man blew out a puff of smoke.

"She wants salt, Pops. She wants salt. She says the soup doesn't have any flavor, and that she wants salt."

I spun around and went to the sideboard to search for the saltshaker. Just as I was about to remove it, I saw the uncovered punch bowl in the center of the table. Without using the ladle, I plunged a glass to the bottom, and, slurping shamelessly, I poured the liquid into the deepest part of my belly. I realized, only when the aftertaste surged up, that it was a little bit sharp. It's the old fucker's fault; he never remembers to put the lid on the punch bowl. I poured myself another drink, what else was I going to do.

to the sands

J'ai tiré ma rouloure
de vie au milieu des sables.

I have spent my miserable
life among the sands.

SAMUEL BECKETT,
Waiting for Godot

I fiddled with the silver dollar, pressing my thumb across the relief. For a moment I felt the urge to tell the Mexican: "It's bad luck. The old lady in Biloxi said it was bad luck." I opened the faucet and drank straight from the tap, water dripping down my neck.

"It's bad luck," I said.

The Mexican kicked the crate. There was a poster of the Virgin of Guadeloupe behind it that was

completely bleached out. I looked back at the table
and wanted to reread the newspaper ad. The Mexican
peeled himself away from the wall and I could see
his red shirt was wet down to his waist. By the time I
wanted to wipe the water off my chin, I was already
confused by the humidity. I heard him clearing his
throat, and I instinctively clenched my dollar until my
fingernails stung.

"*Hermanito*," the Mexican said, "little brother, let's
be reasonable. Let's be *mel-lo*, talk it over."

He lifted the crate gently, reaching into the opening, and without taking his eyes off me, he pulled it up
to the table and sat down, sighing.

"Item one," he said, trying to sound rational,
though he was mumbling, chewing on the words.
"You say it brings bad luck."

By now I had changed my mind. I could almost
guess what he was going to say. I told him:

"I know what point you're going to bring up.
You're going to say: And what do you call this?"

Mexicancityboy scratched the side of his head.

"You're on the right track. What's the answer?"

"I don't know what it's called. But we're fucked."

"Could we be any more fucked?"

"Hardly."

"Later…"

I pointed to the ad.

"There's a problem," I said.

The Mexican raised his eyebrows attentively. I felt like drinking more water.

"Here it says 'price according to type.' What's that mean?"

"It's simple. There are four types A B AB O or one two three four. There's also the negative. Those pay better because they're in short supply."

"And?"

"If you have AB, you get paid double. It's because of the law of supply and demand, you know what I mean? But you'll get paid fifteen."

I caressed my arm.

"How much did you get?"

"Ten. But I'm Mexican."

"And why are they going to give me more? I'm also Latino."

"But you're honey blond. I'm fucked because of my skin. If I toasted myself a little more I could spend my summers in Harlem."

I scratched one of my ears.

"They're going to notice because of my accent."

The Mexican stood up.

"You're right," he said. "We'll have to rehearse it. Stand up."

I let him lead me to the door without making any fuss.

"Now you knock, approach me, and tell me slowly: *Ai laik tu sel sam blad.*"

I opened the door a crack, took a step into the room, and said:

"*Ai laik tu sel sam blad.*"

"*Perfecto.* That's all there is to it."

"Wait," I said. "Suppose they ask me something. Suppose they ask me what kind of blood I have."

"You play dumb, *hermanito*, smile and say: *Ai dont nou.* Let's go over all this again."

I opened the door a crack and stepped into the room:

"*Ai laik tu sel sam blad.*"

"*Wats yuar taip?*"

"*Ai dont nou.*"

The Mexican started to adjust his tie.

"Put your coat on. I'll wait for you by the door."

I put the dollar in my fifth pocket, and before pulling my jacket on, I flattened it out on the mattress with my palms. I dropped a little spit on the old Chianti stain, from when the jacket and I had seen better days.

As I tightened the knot on my tie, I felt like the humidity was going to make me explode at any moment. As soon as I had some dough I'd switch my cigarettes for a carton of milk. You can go into any diner or bar and no drunk is going to deny you a cigarette. But sometimes it's hard to find someone who will treat you to a glass of milk. You feel bad even asking for it. It's not that way with a cigarette.

We went out to Tenth Street, and there'd be no more than fifteen bums on the block, cradled in the doorways holding cans of beer in their hands. We walked to Stuyvesant Place to get the express bus.

"First of all," I said suddenly, "we need to make a life plan."

We moved along trying to catch up to the thin shadow that was falling down the middle of the sidewalk.

"We have a few debts." I introduced the topic.

The Mexican nodded.

"Items?"

"Excluding restaurants?"

"I think so."

"We owe eight in the bodega."

"We pay four. It's better for us to keep our credit open."

I cleared my throat dismally. Even my stride was choking me.

"We have eleven left."

The other one also swallowed hard.

"Eleven," he repeated, distracted. And then, having recovered a little more: "Well, at least that's something, isn't it?"

I had to agree.

"Let's plan it out."

"Rice," Borderboy said. "A bag of rice is cheap and nourishing."

I had some doubts because all the Chinese I knew were skinny, small, and jaundiced. In any case, rice was filling. What you wanted to avoid after all was that feeling in your stomach, as if the air was being yanked out with a rope.

"Beans," I added. "They're cheap by the pound. Besides, if we mix the rice with the beans, we'd have something like a menu item, you know what I mean?"

The Mexican wiped his lips with his wrist.

"You have to balance your diet," he advised. Even if it breaks our hearts, we'll have to buy some sausage."

I gulped.

"Ten for a *daim* each, makes a dollar. A dollar of beans and a dollar of rice: three bucks. We pay the bodega four. That leaves us with eight. Eight dollars."

He looked at the desolation in the expression on my mouth and wiped his nose. He always worked up his courage by blowing his nose.

"It's not so bad," he said. "Think that we'll be able to eat for fifteen days."

"Twenty," I proclaimed. "Twenty if we eat half a sausage a day."

We turned our faces to the side as we passed in front of the Martini pizzeria. As he was about to stop a bus, I grabbed him by the sleeve.

"There's one problem," I said.

"What's wrong? That's the bus to Saint Luke's."

"There's a problem. The silver dollar."

"What about it?"

He patted my pocket to make sure it was still there.

"I was thinking," I said. "Maybe the bus driver won't take it. He might think we're making fun of him. Anyway, I don't know."

"You're right," Border muttered. "We could save the dollar and walk. It's only fifty blocks."

We looked at the concrete courtyards around Stuyvesant Oval that we now had to cross, and the truth is that in that whole area there wasn't enough shade to cover a fingernail. We started walking, thinking about only one thing. Thinking about beer.

After twenty blocks the Mexican started to get metaphysical.

"How's it possible we've sunk so low?" he said.

I was puzzled by the question, not so much because it sophisticated our situation, it defined it categorically, but because we had never been so high up to begin with that we had sunk "so low." For a moment I had the pleasant suspicion that the Mexican had a magnificent past. I'd also had my heyday, as it were, but I'd been in Santiago for two years, which was no fun at all.

"What do you mean?" I asked, even pretending to be offended.

Borderboy didn't wipe his nose this time. That was a sign that a bitter, tango-like period was about to follow. It was his resolve that no longer worked. If things were going so badly, it wasn't such a big deal having a little snot on your cheek.

"Have you by any chance been better off?" I pressed him.

"Much better," he nodded gravely. "I was on a fellowship from September to June. One hundred and twenty. One hundred and twenty dollars a month, they gave me. *Nau finished. Ouver, manito.*"

I was suddenly overcome with incomprehensible dread.

"The rent?" I asked. "It's August, how long has it been since you paid the rent?"

"*Nou problem*," Mexicancityboy said. "The owner *finisht. Ouver.*"

Our conversations would usually stop there. I would ask, he would answer a couple of things, and the matter would be closed. But there were about thirty blocks left, and I became unusually interested in the owner. Before I spoke, I gathered a sort of a *buche*, of the mass of saliva I had accumulated while I was thinking, swishing it into a bulge.

"What do you mean?" I asked. "*Noo mor* on the planet. *Gud bai*?"

"*Nou mor, hermanito.* He emigrated."

"How did he die?"

"Don't fuck around, *fajita*. He died and that's it. Why get all romantic about it now. You die and that's it."

"Like a tourist," I thought. "You're from another country and you're just passing through. Then you go back home."

"But did he get cut? Did they work him over with a blade or something?"

The Mexican shoved his handkerchief inside his shirt collar. He pulled it out and it was wet, then he squeezed it without looking at it, then tossed it in the air, whipping it between his fingers like "Pilate, Pilate."

"He died of old age," he reported. "You're aware of the figure, I presume?"

I shook my head.

"What do you mean?"

"It's like the thousand-dollar question, for fuck's sake. I learned it in high school. The only animal that walks on three legs is man. The old man's cane broke and his forehead smashed against the gutter. *Ouver.*"

I started whistling "Downhill in my defeat the illusions of the past," by Carlos Gardel.

"What about our apartment?" I said finally.

Mexicancityboy rubbed his hands on his pants.

"Unless they come to demolish it because it's a health risk, you can die in it the summer of eighty-eight, and you won't pay a penny. The only thing the police know about the old man is that his name is Rispieri. Nobody knows anybody here. When you die, you won't have anything to worry about. No worries, whatsoever."

Too bad my pal didn't realize the effect his language was having on me. He had no idea how hard my head was working. I could already see myself with a gentle syringe sucking blood out of my arm at St. Luke's, and a blonde nurse, with her apron wrapped snuggly around her little boobs, telling the doctor: "He's not holding it together, Doctor. We're losing him." And the doctor: "Well, let's not waste the fresh supply. Clean him out and then take him down to the morgue. Call his relatives." And the nurse: "It looks like he's not from around here. There's a *pocho* waiting for him in the hallway."

"I'm hungry," I said.

"Well, we're in the same boat, *mano*."

He massaged his stomach, and added:

"And besides, if I'm going to be an asshole about it, you can see that already. I've kind of fallen in love."

"Fuck him," I thought.

"Well, I wouldn't really call her pretty. She's plump, you know what I mean?"

"Chubby," I said.

"Well, I don't know if I'd call her chubby . . . Plump. Good-natured."

"All chubby women are good-natured."

"But this one isn't fat, *boy*. She's just a little meaty. Here, too."

He put his hands over his heart.

"What about the other thing?" I asked.

He put his hands on his belly. He rubbed them a few times across his skin. He was more hungry than in love.

"*It never japen*," he said. "I was supposed to call her up, can you imagine."

"Imagine" meant: a *daim* a call, *tri baks* for the movie, *caple of dolars* a sandwich. He sighed so loudly as he spoke to me that he managed to dry the sweat on my forehead. Let's suppose there are about fifteen blocks to go. I was either deranged or a romantic:

"I'm hungry," I commented. (Romantic.) "I feel weird, I don't know what, having my blood drawn." (Deranged.)

"Money buys eggs," Borderboy said, but he was thinking of something else. He was thinking about the chubby girl he had something going with but *it never japen*. I've been kind of in love myself.

I operate on the basis of contamination. I also had a little sweetheart, but it was spiritual, artistic like that. I was in love with...Ella Fitzgerald. I'm a jazzman. Mohammedan, no longer. I got it from the Mexican. I started to sigh that it was a scandal. That night the black woman was making an appearance at Basin Street East, and you needed a tuxedo or something, to get in. I started to whistle, heartbroken.

"The girl's pretty, you know? She's Cuban." I stopped whistling the melody for five seconds.

"Bring her to the apartment and we'll call the United Nations into session, for fuck's sake."

"She's Cuban all over. Over here..."

The Mexican smacked his ass. It was as if he'd remembered something important.

"A Fidelista, brother. A revolutionary."

For a second I had the feeling that my mouth had stopped producing saliva. I remembered a lecture that a Chilean expedition member had delivered about camels. He'd crossed the desert and the camels carried something like a reservoir of water. A kind of demijohn of water, let's say.

"We should get out of here," I said.

Borderboy wiped his nose. A sign that he attributed a certain amount of importance to the *sabyect*.

"What could we do somewhere else?"

We were coming around the corner, and the hospital was right there.

"The same as here, knucklehead."

"By that you mean?"

"Breathe air out, breathe it in, eat, sleep, and good night. We—"

"—love each other so much..." Mexicali Rose hummed.

"...we're screwed. *Ouver.*"

For Mexican-Hands-Tilling-the-Earth the sight of the hospital was like seeing the eagle on crisp bills. His laughter was bubbling out of him.

"What we have to do..."

"What we have to do," I thought with a little dread.

"What we have to do is leave," my buddy said.

The color drained out of me, as they say in the comics. It wasn't even two weeks ago that I had been at the consul's office tugging on his sleeve and reading the newspapers.

"You're the one who has to make things happen," VivaMexico said.

Me with my stomach like a piggy bank the night before Easter, a die-hard patriotic sentimentalist, I was going to make things happen.

At St. Luke's there was a black receptionist. We felt better. There's a solidarity thing among all the people who are fucked over in New York. Though this doesn't mean you won't starve to death at any moment, for example. Mexicancityboy took care of the blah-blah-blah.

"*Ji want tu sel sam blad,*" he said.

"*Wat color?*" the black man said, showing his teeth.

The Mexican approached me in a panic.

"What's wrong?" I said.

"What color is it?" he asked. "He wants to know what color."

I thought about it for a second.

"Calm down," I ordered him. "The *morocho*," and I nodded at the man's dark skin, "wanted to make a joke. Your sense of humor...*hermanito.*"

He smiled. He walked over to the *morocho* again.

"*Red,*" he said. "*Ji want tu sel sam red blad,*" he said. "*Digmi?*"

"*Ah yes,*" the black man said. "*Regular blad.*"

"*Yes. Regular. Gud yang red blad. Absolutily regular.*"

The black man wrote meticulously in a big volume. That's where he wrote down my name and my age (I told him twenty-two just in case), and noted that I had not been sick. I kept quiet about the pneumonia. My blood was already fucked up enough with all the beer without getting finicky. Behind the counter, he

ordered a little dark-haired nurse to take over. Her
face looked half-Latino, and I spoke to her confiden-
tially in Spanish.

"Do they take a lot out?" I asked.

She turned around, surprised to hear me speak
Spanish. I actually have a bit of a *bolsiflay* face, I look
like a naïve gringo sometimes.

"What do you mean, a lot? What are you asking
me, kiddo?"

I watched her handling the syringe. She plugged
a glass tube into the other one and began to squeeze
it until the air bubbled out of it. And then the girl
said something tremendously philosophical that I'll
remember for all of history.

"That's what our life is like," she said, "nothing
but bubbles. One day some air comes along and blows
them away."

I coughed like it was a party. I thought of a bolero
on the beach in Acapulco drinking gin with coco-
nut juice laying on a balustrade. I had the book of
a famous Argentinean back home. They called him
Borges. I tossed out an extravagant philosophical rant.

"So much masculine vanity, and the only thing
he's good for is gathering flies."

The little brunette smeared a wet cotton swab on the syringe.

"What do you mean?"

I brushed the fingers of my left hand lightly across my eyes.

"Bubbles," I said. And all of a sudden, boom!

I went down to make sure the legs of the examination table were working.

"Lie down here."

I obeyed her, feeling the surface, using the same caution as someone who plunges slowly into the sea in case the water is too shallow. What am I doing here, I said to myself. By now I should be leaving my classes at the Conservatory and on my way to my old man's apartment, and everything would be winter in Santiago, and Mamá would have made some *picarones*, maybe it would have rained, and my little brother would be hanging out in the street with his friends, and I could get into my warm bed, and turn on the record player, and listen to Brubeck's "Rondo à la Turk," and then call up one of my girlfriends on the phone.

"What are you?" the girl asked me. "Argentinian?"

She had helped me roll up my sleeves.

"I'm Chilean. But write down that I'm from Dallas, Texas."

That seemed to please her.

"I listen to Lucho Gatica's records, have you heard of him?"

Lucho Gatica would be nice and cozy in his home in Mexico, playing with his children and Mapita Cortés. Or he'd be happily rehearsing something with José Sabre Marroquín's orchestra at the Odeón studios. I'd never seen him in my life.

"Lucho Gatica," I murmured. "We're close," I added a little louder. "As thick as thieves. Me and Lucho."

She started cleaning my arm and then she thumped my skin looking for the vein.

"Do you have a boyfriend?" I asked.

The girl nodded with her eyes, not moving a muscle.

"I don't," I informed her, "I don't have a girlfriend. Not even for show. *Nazing.*"

I was disappointed that she wasn't excited about my friendship with Gatica. Somehow I had a feeling she would be more gentle with the needle if... And just when she was about to stick me I remembered the days when I had been sick and I was getting my blood drawn all the time so they could take it to the labs. It didn't hurt; I remembered it didn't hurt. It was something else that led me to put the fingernails of my free hand in my mouth and bite on them. It was just that I felt like a whore, excuse my language.

I took advantage of my hands next to my mouth to cover my eyes while I was pretending not to be afraid. Then I rubbed my nose hard. Worse still: the whole operation went into me.

"Relax, kiddo."

I sighed and let my body go. The girl had that thing mothers call the hand of an angel. The syringe filled up in one go, and she made me hold a cotton ball on my arm. She went over to the table and wrote something on a piece of paper.

"Give this to the black guy and he'll pay you."

She saved me the trouble of picking up my sports coat, slinging it over one of my shoulders.

"Thank you," I said, blushing.

The Mexican kept his distance, but he was still keeping an eye on the situation. Fifteen, they paid me. A ten and *faif backs*. He came up to me in the hallway and we went out to the street. I was still clutching the money between my fingers and my jacket was slipping off my shoulders. Mexicancityboy, mother-like, settled it back on for me. I showed him the cash.

"*Hermanito*," he said. You're a real champ. Now let's go to a *dragstore* and get a sandwich."

I threw the cotton swab onto the street and straightened my arm.

"I'm not hungry," I said.

He wiped his nose with his sleeve. The cash had turned him all civilized and shit. He stuffed it into one of his pockets and hummed something.

"What's up with you?" he asked.

There was already shade on the left side of the street. But the humidity wasn't letting up.

"Nothing. Let's have us a sandwich."

We decided on an Italian bodega where they served tagliatelle with heaps of cheese and bologna. For another five cents, you were entitled to a clear and tasteless Chianti. We sat at the counter to save ourselves from having to pay a tip.

"*Hermano*," Borderboy said.

"What?

He put some thought into twisting the noodles onto his fork. First he swallowed hard, and then he stuffed his maw and chewed the whole thing while nodding like a priest.

"You know what's wrong with us?"

I gave him a suspicious look.

"We're going through a moral crisis."

He measured the effect of his phrase out of the corner of his eye as he spread grated cheese over his bread. Italians give Parmesan cheese away for free. Pouring cheese on it was like shoplifting a sandwich. Poor man's tricks. I did the same.

"Aha!" I said.

"A serious moral crisis." He nodded gravely, running his tongue over his gums.

"Hm."

"A serious . . . *serious* crisis," he repeated, savoring the word along with the spaghetti.

I looked at myself in the mirror behind the counter and decided to straighten out my hair.

"Yes," I said.

"We're young, you know? We're missing . . . How can I explain it to you, fella? We need to have fun!"

One day, like in one of those amazing fairy tales, a bird will land on my hair and build its nest there.

"Exactly," I said.

Mexicancityboy licked the corners of his mouth.

"Going out with girls, for example."

"Yes, oh yes."

"Have a few drinks."

"Yes, sir."

"Et cetera."

I finished the rest of my Chianti, asked for the bill.

"Let's go home," I said.

The Mexican furrowed his brow and looked at his fate in the mirror. The crease in his dark skin turned gloomy. Like how a puppy looks, let's say.

"María," he sang. "María works at *Macy's*." I looked at him, unfazed.

"She has a friend. July."

"Gringa?"

"Friendly. *Morocha . . . dark jair*, how you like them."

I was handed the bill. Without giving it any thought I took out a *dolar twenti*.

"Does she speak Spanish?"

"Well, that's a detail, *hermano*."

"Does she speak Spanish?" I persisted.

He curled the vegetation over his sideburns thoughtfully.

"I'll be honest with you," he declared.

I leaned my elbow on the counter and puckered my lips in front of my reflection.

Then what shouldn't have happened at that moment happened. Some teenager had put a coin in

the Wurlitzer and Petula Clark's version of "Downtown" started to play. There were two songs that
week that really got on my nerves. The other one was
"King of the Road" by Roger Williams.

"You're right," I said. "We need to have fun."
The girls would be leaving the store at six. I was the
one, as if I didn't know any better, who stopped the
cab at the corner. With that remarkable intuition
of his, the Mexican whistled the theme softly the
whole ride downtown. He was more fuel than I could
tolerate.

We got some Chesters out of the machine in the
store, and smoked them like Broadway heartthrobs,
squinting our eyes and flicking out a few flecks of
tobacco with the tip of our tongues. We mashed the
butts before getting on the escalator, and Borderboy immediately steered us skillfully to the toy
section.

Now, since it wasn't Christmas or anything like
that, the only thing in the area was a rich old Argentine couple buying a little electric train for the kids.
When María spotted us, all kinds of color went to her
cheeks. There was no doubt that the target on Border
was set. She motioned for us to move away to the children's record section and play the innocent card, as if

we were looking for Cinderella by Mary Poppins, or something like that. I glanced at the other clerk, who smiled at me when our eyes met. Who knows why. Because God is great, I guess. But she was blonde like Budweiser beer and with a waist that wasn't so bad and big teeth. I mean, if I hadn't seen her before, and ran into her on the street, I'd think that the blonde probably worked in a toy store.

"Do you know her?" I elbowed Mexican, who was already finishing another Chester.

He looked up from the records and looked down again discreetly.

"July," he said, swallowing hard. I started breathing faster.

"She doesn't speak Spanish, you said?"

He blinked as he exhaled a puff of cigarette smoke, looking down.

"Not a damn thing."

I swallowed half a liter of spit, desperately rubbing the bone at the back of my skull. This time there was no question: I was in love with July and besides, I was a big asshole. I lowered one hand to my heart and rubbed it intensely, short of breath, feeling some trouble between my legs, and then I grabbed each of

my fingers and squeezed the little bones until they
cracked.

"*Luk!*" I warned Mexican, pretending to be interested in *The Whale Who Could Sing*.

María and July came and stood right in front of
our noses. They had a beautiful smell of pine soap or
something like that. They had just washed and both
wore a layer of makeup this thick. The only thing
left for me to do was to keep from boiling over as
much as possible, and to smile and nod, which makes
you look like a moron or a slimeball. But suddenly I
took her into my arms; I grabbed her on the fly, as
they say. Just at the moment when I was supposed to
smile, open my muzzle, and mumble *plis tu mit yu* so
that no one in the world would hear me, my Philips
lit up, buddy. I moved my jaw forward slightly and,
without saying a word, I looked deep into the bottom
of her eyes and into the bottom of all things with
a bottom, and I told her everything in Chilean but
only with my eyes. Things like *mijita rica, amorcito, yul
see jau i luv yu, my luv.* Something must have happened
then because it was the first time in the history of the
world that a gringa lowered her eyes when she said
jau du yu dú?

She was blonde like that, glossy and warm. That kind of girl who looks like she's still getting out of bed and makes you want to crawl under the warm covers you've just left and rub your nose against her pillow.

Mazatlan Nights did hardly anything different with María. Only that they were talking I don't know what the hell about, but with several hushed parentheticals. The blonde couldn't find any place to hide, so she *espikio ta mi in inglish* all of a sudden.

"*Wat yur neim?*" she said.

"Fernando," I answered without flinching, and my deep voice meant "I so desperately need you."

"Fernando," she said, and looked me in the eyes, and then she began to study her shoes.

Ai sed "yes."

"*Mai neim is July,*" she said then, looking a little above my eyes, somewhere along my forehead.

"*Ai laik it,*" I admitted. And to avoid appearing too much a ruffian, I made a face that could resemble a smile when the time came.

María turned to me and started to adjust my shirt collar. Bad timing: I was a proper mess, as Borderboy used to say.

"Where do you want to go?" she asked.

It was beautiful to feel a pretty lady's fingernails running along your neck. Mexican warned me with his eyes that I shouldn't be too hasty.

"If you don't mind," he said then, "we could go dancing?"

I looked at July, trying to connect with her in the same place where I had hit the mark before.

"No," I said.

"Wat's rong?"

"You talk about dancing but you keep forgetting, *hermano*..."

"What do you mean I keep forgetting! What am I forgetting?"

I pointed a finger at my arm to see if he'd figure it out. With my hand pressed against my thigh I made the *money* gesture. In the dance hall they have the air-conditioning going and they don't serve drinks, I added. "We could..."

I almost cried with pleasure when it occurred to me. That thing they call a conscience, he told me: *"Keep going."*

"We could...?" the Mexican urged me on.

I grabbed a Chester from him, trying not to let my hands shake.

"We could," I said slowly. "Go to Basin Street East to hear Ella Fitzgerald."

The girls put their foreheads together, conferring with each other, and Mexican began to scratch his middle tooth.

María shook out her hair, tossing it over one shoulder.

"We'd have to change our clothes," she said. "It's a fancy place, you know?"

"Let's go like this. It's fancy but it's dark. You tell July to order the drinks in English and that should be enough."

The Mexican put his arm around María's waist and walked a little way ahead. Only his pace had become sluggish. His legs were getting tired.

"*Hermanito*," he said. "You know what to do."

"God does too," I replied.

As soon as we got out of the store, I put my arm around July's shoulders, and the girl made the sort of gesture like someone who's going to rest her hair on your chest, and New York was one big mess, and I liked the whole thing, and I started humming "Downtown," and my legs had gotten all springy and dancy, and when July started talking to me I even understood what she was saying. I mean, my body understood what she was saying. I also jabbered *sam inglish* shooting my arms out like windmill blades, and the four of us had an extensive and rambunctious walk, and we collided with everyone we passed by.

We killed time until eight o'clock, hitting the scotch in an Irish pub, and the girls had bought peanuts from a street vendor and we left the crusty shells wherever we sat. Eventually it became clear that July would be a dancer, and that I would eventually play trumpet in some provincial jazz club. She had a high-roller uncle who'd once made a fortune betting on the Yonkers sulkies, and I had a frustrated penchant for gambling. At the tail end of our second drink, we started putting coins in the Wurlitzer and huddling in a shadowy corner. I began to say pretty things to the blonde and María would translate, and sometimes the Mexican would translate and add things of his own, although all of a sudden he would blunder on and get poetic on me.

By eight o'clock we had finished off the peanuts in a cab, and were going down the steps of Basin Street East, looking like high-class ladies and gentlemen. It was cocktail hour and at almost every table there were busty old ladies with a tremendous tolerance for alcohol. The waiter had our number and seated us at a second- or third-class table behind a banister.

We had two quiet black guys next to us who would take a sip of whiskey from time to time and who were the only ones in the whole place who didn't have cigarettes between their fingers. I thought they might be singers. They never smoke and drink their drinks neat. Onstage, a trio led by a wispy-haired pianist was romanticizing some Cole Porter themes, à la Liberace, though not quite so bitter. July had identified a fleshy writer, with a bruised eye and a head full of curls. She said she had seen him on the cover of a magazine and his name was Norman Mailer, and he had let her down. She said that he'd killed a broad once. I told the Mexican to inform July that I'd read a book by an American named Saroyan and to ask her if he had ever been on the cover of a magazine, and the Mexican said that July said no, but that in another magazine there'd been a picture of a choreographer, Jeffrey, and that she would like to study dance with him, until finally a short man came out on the stage, and that Liberace guy went with his musicians into the bathroom, and the little man's silver hair was crowned in spotlit pink, and he said he felt very proud to present Miss Ella Fitzgerald, and meanwhile a trio of white guys began to pizzicato "Walk Right In" and suddenly Miss Fitzgerald came out all dolled up and I

proceeded to pay homage to her with half the contents
of my glass. July, María, and Mexicali Rose applauded
not as discreetly as the rest of the patrons, and from
then on for half an hour the nightclub was filled with
gurgles, whispers, roller coasters, swings, acts of love,
electricity, laughter that rose like birds and burst into
the bottles, and Miss Fitzgerald's ample breasts were
imperceptibly consuming the air in the room until you
couldn't figure out what to do to pump some air into
your lungs, you couldn't see how or by what right you
existed on the same planet as that woman, you were
the same as a chair, as a broken clock in front of her,
you were a sad thing with burning cheeks, and just
because she existed, Borderboy existed, and María
and July, and my parents in Santiago, and the writer
with curls, and the book I had read by Saroyan, and
the choreographer, and Macy's department store, and
all the blood types and the asylums, and because she
existed people died, and there were millionaires, and
it was good to drink until you lost consciousness, and
the black woman sang "Love for Sale". . .

And suddenly everything was reduced to a simple
form. Ella went into that bathroom, the little guy went
up to the stage, *taim to dans* he said, and the Liberace
guy with the gray hair and the delicate hands came

back, and the black double bass player, and the drummer going *chá-chá* with the drum brushes, and the
big-busted ladies lit more cigarettes, and the gentlemen snapped their fingers asking for the bill, and then
the room became less crowded, and people started
to arrive for dinner. I took out the twelve dollars and
handed it to the waiter, and this time I didn't put my
arm around July's shoulders. This time I squeezed
her waist and let my cheek rest on her head and we
walked outside.

We walked about eight blocks until what had to
happen sooner or later happened. It had to happen at
some point that the Mexican would stop to wait for us
and say, "Well…"

I tapped out the last Chester and squeezed the
empty package with my left hand. That was the city
and the end. There were great plays on Broadway,
fancy bars for late-night hangouts, buses people rode
to visit friends, jazz at the Village Vanguard, fancy
hotels to make love in, angry and funny writers, Latin
American painters on scholarship, marijuana for
a dollar a joint, museums, a zoo on Broadway, TV
shows with Ben Gazzara, Puerto Rican dancers, night
racing in Yonkers, automobiles, there were people.

"Well, well, well, well," the Mexican said.

I smiled, sinking my hands into my pockets.

Borderboy straightened the knot of his tie.

"I'm going to drop María off," he said.

I fingered the coins inside my pocket. As the ele-
phant flies, there would be about seventy cents. *Subway*
for two, thirty. *Subway* for one coming back, fifteen.
Assets: twenty-five cents.

"Perfect," I said. Perfectly. July was holding my
waist.

"*Ji'l teik ker of yu,*" María told her.

They went down the stairs to the subway and left
us there like two more mailboxes on the street, like two
ad posters. Like two shitty water faucets they left us.

"*Wel,*" I said.

I took out the coins and studied them under the
streetlight. Eighty cents exactly. The surplus could be
invested in coffee. In two cups of coffee standing at the
counter of a soda fountain.

"*Want cofi?*" I asked her.

The girl looked me in the eyes. She lifted her
shoulders gently.

I racked my brains to see if there was anything
else I could offer her. In Santiago, Chile, everything
would have been easier. I would have said, "Let's go to
my place," and the girl would have said, "No, take me

home." But here a fella had to be beaten up in English and everything. I didn't even have enough chips in the game to make the slightest move.

"*Mai joum?*" I said, pointing ridiculously toward the Hudson River.

The girl looked down at her shoes.

"*Mai joum?*" I insisted, desperately flapping my elbows, my mouth dry. My face was twitching. There wasn't enough wind to blow away a candy wrapper.

I desperately needed someone to get me out of this movie I'd gotten myself into. To rearrange the scene for me. To have a consuetudinary angel whispering Shakespeare's verses in my ear. I gulped.

"*Vamos,*" the girl said. Like that, let's go in Spanish.

I spent the ride on the express train memorizing the ads on the posters. Lucky for me I had some loose peanuts left in my jacket pocket, and I was able to share them with her. We nibbled them with the tips of our teeth, to see if we could make them last from one station to the next. With the second peanut, I introduced the idea of removing the red husk and endlessly trying to flick it off of my fingers. And after the last nut, I started biting into the shells. We sat in the wicker seats in the center of the subway car and we didn't matter to anyone. I started humming

"Downtown," and the girl pulled a scarf out of her purse and motioned for me to help tie it for her. Then she smiled at me like in a shitty romantic movie with Gregory Peck and Audrey Hepburn. And it wasn't that the scene was lousy rotten or anything, but that I was supposed to say something so tremendous in the style of *ai lav yu madli*, and the fucked-up thing was that I wasn't in character. I'd been suspecting for a while that this wasn't a Technicolor musical that would end with Doris Day pregnant in a suburban house, a job with a thousand a month, and blond children with blue eyes, but rather one of those modern Italian ones where everything ends up in the same shit, and the assholes go down some alley filled with rocks and potholes, on a cloudy day, smoking a joint and freezing to death.

Our apartment had just one advantage compared to others in the neighborhood. It didn't smell as much like urine or dishwater as it did of paint or solvent from the construction sites where the Mexican was working. He had started making colored boxes, which he knew would one day be bought by the director of the Museum of Modern Art or by some philanthropic millionaire. I moved like a bat in the dark, and before turning on the light bulb I threw my Mapuche poncho over the gray sheets. In some movie, the leading actor would have delicately maneuvered the indirect light of a Chinese lamp, and would have taken out ice cubes and some hallowed bottle. I started whistling "Downtown" to ease my nerves. I turned on the light, what else was I going to do.

The girl blinked at the bare bulb, and she looked pink and clean. I smiled as if asking her to forgive my stupid hands in my pockets. And then I was jealous of the Mexican because she went over to his boxes and said *biutiful*. The only charming thing I had was the brass trumpet above the bed, but any two-bit soldier could have played it better than I could. Besides, Herb Alpert's band was becoming popular, and there wasn't a teenager who didn't know how to distinguish between some random bray and his music. For a moment I thought she had come because she was drunk as an Irish cabby.

I sat on the bed, and leaned my head against the wall. She took off her scarf and came over and sat next to me. I put my arm around her shoulders and stared at the wall. My legs were trembling and my lips parted. I was sweating like a chicken on a spit.

Then I lifted my mouth to her cheek, then swept it over her lips and probed the taste of her perspiring skin with my tongue. I noticed that the girl was gently bringing a hand to my hip and stretching her warm tongue between my lips and licking my left lobe and then my temple, and then she was slowly licking across my face and moved down to lick the hair on my chest as my hand dipped between her hot thighs.

"*Weit*," she whispered. She tugged off her panties and bra, and as she kneeled on the poncho she brought her small breasts close to my lips. When I leaned in to kiss them, to sink my nose into the warm cavity they created, she began to kiss my hair and forehead.

Slowly I started getting the idea. It was wonderful. We were licking each other.

"*Ai felt sou lounly*," July said, descending my naked back, her mouth full of saliva. My eyes were half-closed, searching for her belly so I could kiss it. I wrapped my arms around her waist and we lay with our faces on the pillow looking at each other.

"I understood what you said," I said, squeezing the back of her neck. "You said that you felt lonely. Do you understand me?"

She nodded with her eyelashes and a smile. Delicate but hot, too.

"You're with me now," I said, my chin nudging her chest. I cupped her breasts and put my knee between her legs. "Do you understand me?"

"Yes," she replied.

"You can spend the night here."

"Yes."

I slowly pushed my member between her thighs, and penetrated her. Everything was good: the smell of the paint thinner, Border's boxes, the roughness of the poncho.

That's when we really made love. First barely moving, as if exchanging Christmas gifts, memories, her tongue panting slowly, me speechless.

Then I pulled the lamp cord and we caressed each other to sleep. Before that I learned a lot from her back, and from her thighs, and from the soft swell of the curve of her ass. She had repeatedly groped my legs. And my jaw.

When I woke up, the light was filtering through the sheets of newspaper that covered the only window. Everything in the room was arranged in a mess that I was familiar with. The trumpet beside the pillow, the Mexican's boxes scattered on the floor, July's hand flaccid on my hip. I stood up silently, and smiled as I put on my pants. I extracted the silver dollar from my fifth pocket, and bet my fortune on a heads or tails. I opened my palms and studied the coin almost without giving any thought to the outcome. Combing my shaggy hair beside the window, I wet my dry lips with my tongue. Then I buttoned up my shirt and went down to the street.

I bought a carton of milk, a loaf of French bread which I bit the end off of, and two bags of tea. I invested the change in a plastic container of peach jam. It would be hotter than yesterday: even the birds seemed stunned.

July woke up when I bumped into the door. She watched me look at her and covered herself, pulling the poncho up over her eyebrows. I went to the stove and boiled the milk, thinking about the flame. I meticulously rinsed the only two cups we had, and spread jam on the slices of bread, silently. Even though I wasn't looking, I could sense how July was putting on each piece of her clothing.

We sat on the edge of the bed, and we savored the hot, sweet milk, without speaking to each other. Then July picked up her purse, teased the hair over her forehead, parting it slightly with her fingers, and cleared her throat before speaking.

"*Werk*," she said.

I got up to open the door for her.

"Your house," I told her.

And I pointed to the humidity-cracked walls.

I watched her walk away toward the entrance to the subway, and immediately sat down on the bench to look at the buildings in front of me. I still had a piece of French bread in my hand, and the thick mar-malade was dripping down the edges. I put the piece of bread in my mouth, and I chewed it for a long time, until I felt it move down my throat and settle into the bottom of my stomach.

basketball

for Loreto Herman

I discovered the tango through an unsteady uncle
who would lay siege to the house on Thursdays
when some money would fall into his hands and
minced meat would be added to the softly stringy
Yugoslavian noodles, as well as prunes and cheese.

I was an outsider at the parties; had friendly
exchanges with the wallpaper in the corners; I was
a sort of Nat King Cole in making my voice velvety
when talking to the girls, and a habitual eater of cakes.

The coach of the school team had given me the
cold shoulder. Even though my aim was fierce, even
though I was able to make a basket from outside the
key with the same acuity a pigeon lands on the eaves
of a church, or with that same soft snap of pulling
on wool socks, that movie actor thing fucked up my
reputation, that unrelenting eagerness to gratify my

vanity, to remember some fancy dribble when there were only three minutes left and we were losing. The coach had noticed the dark circles under my eyes, and he thumped my liver, and asked me if it was sore here, it looks like you are sick. When he caught me one night sucking on a beer with the homos at the Bier Hall, he tried to set up an intervention with my parents. But my old man was working hard at the party, the cops had bashed his head in, and he was walking around with a gash from that. So he didn't share his grand epiphany, and even I started to get used to squandering my time cutting school. But nothing too cheerful, buddy, just going around and around downtown, just going to Radar or Rolec at ten in the morning with a quince jelly and a piece of bread and butter to listen to Gatica records and the first Ray Charles songs, which were out of this world. Of course, the old guy in gym class got into a fix with the head teacher, who taught us philosophy, and who kept me on my toes because I had read Kafka and wore my hair a little too long and all that. When he caught me putting up a poster of Fidel on the school's newspaper wall, he took the case to the school board, from which I was honorably absolved.

The music that you could hear then was by some affectionate black guys, the Platters they called them,

Giolito had a trio more dull than a Sunday without
soccer, and the jazz club was in Merced, near the
Santiago Theater, and that's where I got my oxygen
and my blood, but never a girl; there the girls had
those long dresses that sanded down their waists, and
any leftover roughness was filed off by the sticky hands
of the conceited little snobs who had enough dough
to get some of that gin with gin, those first batches of
marijuana, and above all, that thing so inaccessible, so
remote, so close to impossible bliss, that thing called
the moped.

Conclusion, my friend Jaime who first huffed
Brahms through a deafening whistle he made with his
knuckles had gotten a clarinet, or maybe the mouth-
piece of a clarinet, and if you put a little goodwill in
your ear, and if you listened really closely, you could
identify "Basin Street" as the swill he was playing
and I swelled up from hitting the pans so much,
and seeing that I was going nowhere as a vocalist,
because this guy Calvo had lent me Billy Eckstine's
long-play, I understood that there was nothing else
I could do, patience. Then I fell madly in love with
a girl from Quinta Normal, super spiritual, the girl,
like she didn't want to have anything to do with a
bed, I had a pataphysical discovery (forgive me), about

the je ne sais quoi of basketball, and I discovered I
loved skin more than anything else in this galaxy.
There was nothing left for me to do but to be a writer,
goddamnit. So I put on my grandfather's long scarf,
broke off relations with my hairdresser for good, and
convinced Jaime that we should enroll in the Arrow
Sports Club on General Velásquez Street.

That's when we got grabbed by a brilliant guy who
if you haven't heard of him your life up to this point
has been worthless, his name was motherfucking Jara-
millo damn it. When he saw my build and studied my
hands, he said: "I'll put you in at center forward." And
indeed, I could do a somersault with the ball in my
right hand in front of players with the tightest skills,
and my body would continue on in unbroken balance.
They put me up against Tito Salazar, the tenor Yan-
coli, and finally Flaco Alcayaga and I swear to God,
I made them dizzy with the smell of leather. Tight
beneath my phalanges, the ball was as compliant as
a lung, it pounced like a cat, its hard fibers became a
feather beneath my fingers; I did nothing, my hand
commanded, my back twisted, my sphincter contracted, my legs clenched and unclenched as if I were
just a shadow; in an instant I was free of all my op-
ponents and my bird, my lark, my little shitty pigeon,

would shoot out and gently sink into the basket. I could have written a novel during our workouts; the only bad thing was that Erika was leery of the bed, she was miserly about the rubbing of her breasts as if she were a sacred Hindu heifer and all that, and I had no vocabulary, I was pure stink inflated with silence, pure synopsis, and I wasn't making my formal debut in any bed, and if things continued like that I might even turn gayer than a handbag full of rainbows.

Second part, Team Arrow came out a cool fifth in the neighborhood championships. The Slaughterhouse crew, the Gustavo Helfmann crew, the Cerrillos Boys, the Metallurgists, and the team from Recorrido 4 Alameda General Velásquez walked all over us.

We defeated Fumblers by disqualification, and beat Night School Number Twelve, and the Socialist Sports Club. If this doesn't tell you anything, you should know that for the last two years Arrow has been the irremediable bottom dweller. I scored whenever they asked me to, but it was on defense where I tripped over the broom, and all because I still kept angling for beer: the dark circles under my eyes were flourishing, my morale was starting to get screwed by having snuck out of school without telling the old man, and I no longer had the wind to cover my zone.

But from half-court on I was one of the most definitive things you've ever seen in basketball. Jaime, who was the only one who knew the intimate details of my life, used to secretly call me "the basketball virgin." And what I was most envious of was that he had gobbled up a Freud book for a psychology paper and treated me like a psychopath or something like that.

He told me I was sublimating myself, you see.

And maybe he was right, because ten minutes into the game I was starting to have trouble with those tight shorts. Then I had to turn my back to the stands, or call for the ball in the middle of the attack to cover myself midleg for a minute, what else was I going to do. And one day that thing you're all thinking about actually happened.

Meanwhile, what you usually find in Santiago winters are orange trees, milk sold in glass bottles left on the sidewalk drug over with peelings and pieces of paper among other things.

To the point: that winter Sunday offered me an angel's introduction. I woke up half-mystical, almost lucid, and when I cleaned the saucepan the burner smelled like the Holy Spirit, at least like a dove, and there wasn't even a hint of sun, just tight clouds, like a freight train, and the truth is that as soon as I went out to the street I was done for or something along those lines. The worst part about it was that the night before I had cooked the thing with mineral water, listening to those Mozart songs where it's always the same thing, *para-pa-rá-chipún-chipún*, and reading a sleepy Zane Grey which I got completely wrong. So in half an hour I was already good night sheep. After getting dressed and grabbing the ball, so to speak, I walked past a church where there were two guys beating each other up. The owner of the soda fountain on the corner threw out a little drunk guy, and on the border between Saturday and early Sunday morning I was the very image of little baby Jesus of Prague that was inside the local dance club. While I was dialing Erika's number, a lippy little whore grabbed ahold of my jacket. I tried to be as much of an asshole as I could and asked her what I could get her, a glass of milk or something. And what she wanted was a glass of milk, so she went and drank it at the counter, making faces at me. I called Erika, who took a while to get to the phone because she was coupling a chicken, as she told me later, and I told her to meet me at the court, that it was a matter of life and death. I must have sounded awful because she didn't ask me if I was drunk or anything. Then I had some problems with a little tramp who wanted to steal my ball from the top of a stool and tried to roll it across the tile floor.

I got off the bus at Central Station and ran to the court where Arrow plays, bouncing the ball as if my hands were magnetic. Although it could have been a dream I had while I was running. If it had been a dream, it went like this: I was running, bouncing a ball through deserted streets, and I wasn't breathing or anything like that, maybe I wasn't even running; but the leather of the ball was sweating compliantly, and it folded back around my skin like a beast, and it compressed into my hand, and licked my fingers; it was the same as feeling how a flower germinates, and as it passed through the air it burst open, but somehow when it came back to my hand it was once again solid. And suddenly the whole street was a single convulsion, the ball was licking the sidewalk, it was beginning to unravel what was below every boundary, only the rhythm was safe and nothing else remained, it was like Coltrane's records with Elvin Jones, Coltrane was everywhere, he trafficked in chaos, he carried things until he scorched them, he massacred all order, Jones clenched the expansion, Jones was a big prick, Jones was a lady, so many moonlit nights, so much tide and embossment, so much blood quota.

In the locker rooms I noticed the cement was damp and ants were moving through the slits in the door, circulating through the cracks, and in the gloom a spider's web was swaying. Someone had sprinkled the floor with apple peels, but someone had also put all that silence in the morning so that no one would know what to do with their hands, and I forgot my mother's face, my first house, the first loneliness in a shabby building by the railroad tracks from San Antonio to Cartagena one summer.

I put on my sneakers, the orange T-shirt with the black fifteen embroidered small on the chest and big on the back and walked leisurely to the middle of the court. Before I warmed up my forearms and brushed my thumbs over the edge of my eyebrows, before I could inhale deeply the full roundness of the ball, I knew I would make the shot even if I didn't look. So I sat on the ball, and I was looking at my knees the whole time I was inside the circle.

When Erika surprised me, I felt a kind of fire igniting in my shoulder. I gathered my meager flames, my parochial bones, set the true limit between my two ears, and went about straining out my words, even though I was so mute, so certainly incognito on the planet, with sharp elbows and supple phalanxes. I was going to push Erika down on my prick along the left side until her thighs popped open with my knee, until she had to ask me to do it in the name of the Holy Father, of all Jehovah's Witnesses, in the name of every good and false prophet that has ever inhabited the galaxy. I who didn't want to die was willing to raise a toast to death. As if my hand had become enormous and I could break a neck or crush a ball with my bare hand, crush a jugular or bash my head against the post under the basket.

"What's wrong with you?" she asked, her eyes bulging as if someone were pulling them out of her head. Above her chestnut-colored cluster of hair, above her stern, donkey-like forelock, the sun was already turning her into a kind of archangel. The rest of the light was there just to fuck with my eyes. I got up, and the dream should have ended there: I was breathing again, but *pam-pam-pam*, like something kicking. It didn't even occur to me to take my shirt off to cover my crotch. If she came to kiss me seriously (I could glimpse it in the way she was softening her eyelids), if she put flesh to flesh with her lip and my muzzle, the party was over for her. Over: the name, the name of her father, that little evangelical guitar player she liked to listen to so much in Quinta with Lord I'm going to your kingdom, and it didn't matter if it was Erika, the princess of the Quinta neighborhood with her perky breasts and hot thighs, it could have been Olga who lived on the first block on Manuel Montt, who got so velvety with the records of the Four Aces and made you feel her hips like a swaying in your own belly, or Angélica, who was always too pale to go through with the ultimate holocaust, or little Gloria, who locked herself up in the toilets of the hosts of those who threw our fifth-grade parties to cry over lost lovers.

I grabbed the kiss out of the air, and there I set the first trap for her with my tooth, without giving her time to breathe, and then I pushed hard on the kiss to get it down her throat, to sow it in whatever part of her flesh where her hand was raised, turning into a fingernail in her lover's ribs. "I'm in love," I told her.

"How does it feel?"

She allowed me to munch on the hair above her ear. All the foliage was falling with the sun, a bird was rushing about, my neck ache swayed, the holes in my nostrils clogged with hair. And her mouth was wet, and my perfectly dry lips were a single crack, a snout of sawdust, of a doll, I was afraid of hurting her

with all my rubbing, but the moisture of her gums
was making them fertile, I had all the words I needed
to baffle her, at any moment I would begin to levi-
tate, with my blood pulling me toward the strands of
her hair, it was as if the whole sky was a magnetized
fever, but the words swelled my neck and diaphragm,
something was missing to put them in order, someone
to squeeze my muzzle to modulate them. I could reply
"an immense sweetness," "a massacre," "some rage."

Grab my ribs, my panting said, loosen my shorts
with your fingernails, now bite my shirt, lick your
tongue down my shoulder, let's go beyond my throat,
beyond my eyebrows, beyond my knees, beyond this
asphyxiation, Erika, this space that will see itself
warped behind your haunches made into a great bed,
a carpet of air, you and I will make an era, we'll levi-
tate raised by the whirlwind and everything will happen in the air, crashing against the birds, crushing the
same insects in their own territory, like bees, like dogs,
like angels. But Erika wanted me dead, she wasn't
going to allow any more negotiations than pastries
and invitations to the movies, than dancing on Saturday afternoons and Roberto Inglez with only one
finger and the Four fucking Aces, and for me to simply
give in, my hands hot, my tufts of hair upturned, my

neck bent into a baseless river, a pure village stream to dip my paws in, outrage her with softly calloused skin, delicate female protuberances, and then scream out, towel dry, turn up the radio, chew a sandwich, buy Liberty cigars, chat with the younger brother, tidy up the fold of her skirt... If only she had asked me again how it felt!

And suddenly, solidly, compactly our heads crashed against the tree. If she didn't scream it was because I covered her tongue with my mouth, and the tree bark released that spurt on her cheek, and it was the ants that went over my neck and clambered into my ear, and what did her hands want, to pulverize my liver, to make my lungs transparent, torque those hard veins, almost broken, almost sweaty, or I was dealing with her and her face was violet and it was yellow and it was pinkish, and there was a way the asphalt spoke, a way the sun spoke, a way the trees burst without moving a leaf, standing, sweating, and I let go of her lips, I put my hand around her waist so that she would live, so that she would submissively bend her loins and her breasts to the sun, but I didn't want her freedom, it's as if she was going to vomit it over my shoulder, more blood was going to come out of her eyes, her wet nostrils were going to spill out her congestion, her ears were going to fall off in pieces covered with ants (you were going to die Erika like a stupid flower, like an unharmed navel), and I put my hands against the back of her neck, and she kicked me between the legs, she armed herself with teeth, she armed herself with spittle, her breasts were as hard as a knuckle blow to the head, she kicked and I walloped her head against the trunk, as if in self-defense, in the last throes I was pushing my nails through her hair, crushing her forehead, and her sweat was covering the coarseness of the wood, her nose was splitting, her lips were about to burst, and then I let her go, I was too weepy to go on living, the pain between my legs was shrieking, as if she had made her definitive stroke, implementing the cruelest finishing touch she planted my tongue in the cement, she wanted me to fornicate with the rough granules of concrete, with the pulverized rubber of every sneaker that had been there, with teeth broken against a sterile mouth, she wanted to see me crying, she wanted to follow her offer to the sun, her own crying, her cheekbone torn, her black hair damp, the edges of her breasts wet, bitten, degraded, she wanted to leave, she was leaving, and I was a flawless ending, almost a queer, a definite virgin, absent, the rotting dust in my nostrils, that sad useless hardness down there.

Then Erika must have left, and I might have
been rubbing my eyebrows with my fingertips, or my
fingernails were in my mouth so no one would see me
crying, or Erika was there and the sun was flooding
between eyelash and eyelash and my tears were boiling me blind. I felt a shadow coming out from under
the concrete, an overhang that was just beginning to
wet my ankles, a slow curtain, like a final act of a very
bad play where the protagonists remain static searching for the drama in the inane, as if the stone, the
twitching eye, contained an action that had better not
go anywhere, since they are going to end the play with
the death of this servant speaking, and all of you are
going to go out to the foyer to smoke a cigarette.

That was my shadow, devoted especially to freezing my legs, covering the curly hairs, unrushed, and
my belly after all this was withdrawing even though
the sun was looking for me, as if it were a knife, I
suppose, as if my belly were not some unfinished
symphony or that quarrel were a last tango or an old-
fashioned song, or a murder in some sluice. Fucking
hell, I was beginning to savor the stone: to rub my
nose sweetly against the layer of dust that was opening up into some simple and indecipherable design.
The tears above the hair on my upper lip tasted

magnificent. I pulled them down over my teeth with
the tip of my tongue, began to scrape my gums with
my fingernails, to feel my cheekbones, and everything
felt hot, freshly bloomed, ridiculous, chubby, comical.
And my sex was also amusing me, so curled up, a dead
little fly, a poor hypochondriac slug that had failed in its
best act, in front of the stage of all my ghosts, in front of
Samuel Bennet for example, in front of Holden Caul-
field, in front of Chet Baker, Gerry Mulligan, Coltrane,
João and Astrud Gilberto, Dorival Caymmi, Julio Sosa,
in front of my vigorous hard-ass grandparents, in front
of so many sick conversations in penumbral nightclubs,
so many breasts intuited and never caressed, in front of
my successful friends, Golden a 7 out of 10 in Biology
and Medicine, Carvallo a 7 in Mathematics and Archi-
tecture, Villanueva another 7 in Gymnastics and on to
top marks at the U of Chile, in front of all the parents
who surprised us a little further into the kiss on dilapi-
dated sofas on all those cobblestone streets of Santiago,
in front of the shameful dead nights, you imbeciles,
with a magazine in hand and the stained tiles, and then
I retreated, huddling over a center I didn't have, running away from shadow's shit talk, and out of the same
weeping grimace I was slowly sharpening my smile,
I was closing my eyes, I was falling asleep, my knees

against my chest, animal, definitive, one more beast on
the planet, like that tree, that dry grass.

I woke up when the asphalt was white. The shade
had crept across my back and gone on to spill over
the pile of bricks behind the bush. I needed to drink
water, but my legs were stiff, preventing me from moving. I slowly started to move them, offered myself up
to the sun until the skin below my knees yielded. Then
I tried to get up by leaning my hip against the ground,
and then my hand, and then I twisted my back,
and that's when I was caught in the full turbulent
sea of light and had to bend my neck over my shirt.
Kneeling down, I was conscientious, ran my tongue
over my lips, spit on my hands and wet my forehead,
cheekbones, and eyes a little. I tilted my gaze almost
covertly to catch the sun straight above my head.
Stumbling, eyes downcast, the light skittering across
my shoulders like persistent rain, I went to the center
of the court to pick up the ball.

Touching the leather gave me some relief. The
entirety of the sun had gathered upon it, a little bump
was sticking out of it near the valve, and I had trouble grabbing it and wrapping it completely inside my
taut fingers. Then I looked for the hoop, the grave
mesh framework unbroken in space, with no wind,

no music, no birds, no spectators, no foliage noise, no music from nearby houses. I had the foolish sensation that I could not taint that silence. When the hems of my shorts brushed against each other, I twisted my neck, afraid that someone would come to reprimand me. Almost without noticing it, I squatted down and, without bouncing the ball like I usually did, my arms went back, retracted gently like someone who collects fish in the ocean, among the rocks a string of sardines, and all the air chapped by the sun shudders with what gushes in the wake. And I was rising up with the movement, I knew my ankles were lifting off the court in a harmonious but definitive way, and my hands were suspended in space and my eyes danced from the circle to the hoop.

The ball bobbed around inside the net.

I had forgotten how it sounded when it dropped to the asphalt; I don't know if it ever fell or if it remained tethered to the net the whole time until the game against Ferroviarios was played, or if it bounced around violently and crashed against the bleachers, or if it exploded in the air and the rim was pulverized in its fall.

I moved my whole sad sunstroke to the locker rooms. I was spitting through my teeth as I skirted the silence of the zone, with my fingers intertwined above my hips, on that part of the skin Bachiller Tudanca called the area bordering the rump. And then I had this foolish desire to put on a black shirt, a tie decorated with multicolored fish and birds, a suit fit for a pimp, and go see a girl in the Fine Arts workshop and all at Dardignac and Pío Nono. And then buy movie tickets and go see the revival of *Champagne for Caesar* with Ronald Colman, or *The Snows of Kilimanjaro*, which was by Hemingway and whatnot. And then go play Ping-Pong at the party headquarters and talk insanely about Fidel to those dudes at the Pedagogical Center, such smooth talkers those guys. And then go to the Bier Hall to listen to Tito Campbell singing that thing about I can't give you nothing but love, baby, that's all I can give you, drink beer *jusque à tomber*, as the French say.

Therefore, since I had a scenario for the afternoon, I even felt awful seeing Erika sitting on the bench, tangling all her loose hair around her fingertips. I tried to adjust my package, and raise my eyebrow a little, and brush the muck that was coming out of my nostrils away with the back of my hand, because it's not customary to walk around so unrefined, so *cuma*, so sleazy in front of a girl, no matter how much of a virgin you are, et cetera.

But something unbelievable happened to me,
bosom buddy. Besides the color, the ball, all that summer coating that was by itself making contact with my
whole body, including that, all the tangos by Mores,
Sosa, and Rivero that I could have sung admirably
in that very second, even if I decided to exhale all the
air from my lungs, besides all that, I became so pro-
foundly sad, so ashamed, with my hands crossed over
my shorts, that I looked her in the eyes and smiled at
her, as if one of those Hollywood assholes were filming
us for CinemaScope. But the truth is that neither she
nor I was good enough for more than a neighborhood
newspaper, not even for an hour and twenty minutes
of reel, maybe at most for a little synopsis between a
John Wayne film with Robert Mitchum and a Mel
Ferrer film with Audrey Hepburn, we weren't even
good enough for a sticker, nor for a note in the margin
of a novel; if God had existed and was a novelist, or
a screenwriter of a film that he has in his head and
doesn't tell it to the actors, like Antonioni for example,
he would have taken advantage of that moment to
take a nap or smoke a cigarette or phone a soulmate
to tell him those ridiculous things that we talk about
with our soulmates. I mean . . . that if someday they
show this movie in heaven, and you get to see it, even

if God who is everywhere (as those who have seen him say) had captured this piece of pure good people, the guy who does the editing in the lab would have cut the pieces of our scene and would have given them to the children who need a piece of celluloid to watch the eclipses.

She called my name and let her hair down.

Even a little breeze came up at that moment, filling her eyelashes with dust. Come to think of it, all that was missing were Mantovani's violins or something like that, I guess.

"Are you serious?" she said.

I shrugged my shoulders and furrowed my eyebrows tightly.

"Am I serious about what?"

"What you said before."

My mug was cracked and her lips were moist. It was like a return to the prehistoric times of our life.

"What did I say?"

"What you said to me out there on the court."

"When?"

"Well, when...you kissed me."

I wanted to tell her that I hadn't kissed her...I wanted to tell her that it had all just been an assassination attempt.

"I don't remember," I grunted, staring at her cleavage again.

"So it wasn't true."

I became positively furious. I didn't mind lifting my hands from my shorts or anything like that, nor did I mind my little bird flying away if it was necessary. I had to have the palm of one hand open, in order to grab the unloaded punch from the other hand.

"It was true, goddamnit! It was absolutely true, Erika Garcia!"

"What was true?"

"What do you mean, what was true? What I told you out there on the court."

And as if all that existed in the galaxy were a waltz or a tango orchestrated by Mores, or Piazzolla or the typical D'Arienzo, or a foxtrot from 1920, I grabbed her by the waist and took her to the locker rooms, I swear on my mother's life.

I don't know which hand I used to stretch out the mat, nor with what pain of hers I penetrated her, nor how the angel began to tear into me, nor to what point my ribs were split apart when all that smell entered me, and that sharp moisture appeared between her thighs, nor do I remember the kisses, the sign of the zodiac, the lunar phase, the angle of the sun on the wall.

I'm sure it took her half an hour before she pulled down her skirt, tucked her tangle of hair into some kind of order over her ears, and finally covered the stew of black paint around her eyelids with her fingertips. At that exact moment I felt an overwhelming urge to put my pants on and throw my shirt over the Team Arrow's glorious Virgin Mary.

"What should we do?" Erika asked.

She was shaking out her skirt and still looked very amorous and her voice was raspy, like Greta Garbo, as it were.

"What do you mean, what should we do?"

"What should we do now?"

I looked around the entire locker room for the answer. I immediately threw my jacket over my head.

"I don't know. I'm hungry."

Erika made one of those movements that young ladies use to adjust what they have on their chests.

"Me too," she said.

I scratched my stomach, overjoyed.

"To tell you the truth, I am really hungry. It must be lunchtime."

"Let's have lunch at my house."

149

I gave myself a little time to scratch my nose and some time to stare at her.

"What do you have?"

"What do you mean, what do I have?"

"What do you have to eat?"

She finished adjusting a ribbon that gathered the rest of her disheveled hair into a bun. I made a piece of newspaper flit away from above her right temple with the tips of my fingers.

"Chicken."

"Chicken with what?"

"With mashed potatoes and salad."

"All right," I said. "Let's go."

I grabbed the ball and we walked to the exit. Almost as soon as we stepped outside, I grabbed her by the elbow and turned her around.

"Wait a second," I told her. "I want you to see something."

I moved forward a few feet bouncing the ball until I was inside the key, and neatly placed my feet on the free-throw line.

"Now, watch carefully," I instructed her with a nod.

I put the ball between my legs and propelled it with all the gentleness in the world, as if I were sending off a ship in Valparaiso, a ship that could be going anywhere in the world. The ball went over the backboard and was lost somewhere in the gravel at the back of the court. I never played basketball again. Years later I published a book of short stories, and I just recently finished writing my first novel.

To Erika I said: "Let's go eat that chicken."

first year, elementary

My brother takes the two straps and crosses them through the buckle of the leather suitcase he bought especially for this trip. The old lady yelled at me from the kitchen to tell him to pack his galoshes for when it rains. When I told him he dismissed me with an indifferent wave of his hand.

"They'll only be a nuisance," he said. "Besides, it's summer there. It doesn't rain there."

I went to the kitchen and she kept insisting. She doesn't believe a place exists where it doesn't rain. My old lady's always making sure that you don't get sick, all day long she keeps telling you that your socks are wet, that you're sweaty, that you should always keep the door closed because of the draft. Mamá is inclined to confuse a cold with leukemia.

She's like the old ladies in Italian movies, good in the kitchen and she pampers the kids. My old man is also like dads in the movies, and he's a damn fantastic old man, with a heart that good. My old man is always giving his coat away in the dead of winter and then he has to buy another one on credit. A crazy flower of a person my *papito* is.

I have a feeling that today is going to take the cake, because as Italian as my folks are, it's funny that they've barricaded themselves in the kitchen and don't want to say goodbye to my brother. My old man said no way in hell would he say goodbye to him because they had a fight last night and my mom told me that the old man had told my brother that he was a son of a bitch. I think that she's barricaded in the kitchen out of sheer solidarity, while my brother is getting all worked up pressing the other suitcase shut.

We were sitting on the bed smoking, watching him. I spend all my time smoking. That's another thing that drives my *mami* crazy. She calls me a *pendejo*, says that I'm always going to be an asshole and small and that I'm not going to be like my brother, who's super smart and elegant and buys his jackets in a little posh store in Providencia. Mami can't stand to see me with a cigarette hanging out of my mouth. The other one smoking next to me is Paula, who's kind of like my brother's girlfriend. We're in my room and not his because my brother doesn't like to mess around in his bedroom: he says my room has more ambience. He calls all my books and records and the posters I put on the walls ambience. My brother thinks that rooms filled with books are great places to bring good-looking chicks. He's never bought any books or records because he spends his dough on dressing like an asshole, with Italian ties and suits practically tailored across his back. I'm the opposite, wandering around like a tramp and with hair that looks like this. Hair's the other thing that irritates the fuck out of my old lady.

My brother closes his suitcases, calculates their weight, adjusts some loose straps, and then puts them on the floor, apparently satisfied with his work. I think my brother is so upset about this thing that my parents told him, that they're not going to say goodbye to him, that he's decided to get cultured. That's why he walks over to the bookshelf and checks out my books by running a finger over them. Then he takes one off the shelf, dusts it off by slapping it against his thigh, lifts it up, and even looks as if he were reading through it. He must be about to faint from all the intellectual effort he's exerting. He pauses on a page and even seems to be reading it. Although it's not very bright in here, I'll be damned if that red book with the black title isn't *Of Time and the River*, by Thomas Wolfe. Paula has raised the blind a little and is looking out at the street. Not that I'm really observing from here, but there's no doubt that it's raining. It's just that as Paula's standing there, she has her neck twisted as if it were raining.

"Did you read this one?"

I'm about to tell him no, so he won't take it with him. My brother's one of those guys who think that once you read a book you can throw it away. He thinks that reading a book is the same thing as going to see a movie. Besides, I want to be a writer and I collect them. My old woman said to me: a longhair, smoker, pothead, and now a writer: *ecco un figlio maricone*.

In the end I don't say no. I try to look him in the eye to tell him that it's a good book, that it's a blood-curdlingly good book, and that it matters to me right here in the nut sack if he reads it or not. That I don't care if he takes it. But this *huevón*, this idiot, never looks anyone in the eye. He's always half-smiling and self-conscious about his nose. I don't know if it makes any sense to say that his whole face converges on his nose.

"Yeah I read it," I tell him.

"Can I borrow it?"

"Take it."

He sits in a chair and looks around at the walls and ceiling of the room. This is the tenth time in the last ten minutes that I've seen him look at his watch.

"There's still time," he says.

The three of us are silent. I hope an ant doesn't walk by because it would scare the hell out of us. Paula changes position, leaves the blinds, and looks around for my brother. His gaze is fixed on the wall, and I don't know where else he intends to look. I've already shaken another cig into my hands and I light it. I walk over to the door. Deep down, all I want to do is get the hell out of there and away from all this. I just wish this day were already over. I'd like to have it crossed off the calendar. But he stops me in the doorway, calling me what he used to call me when I was a kid.

"Talk to them again," he tells me.

I get a little closer to see if he rolled his eyes when he said this. If he moved his eyes around when he asked me for it. I move closer to see if he's watching me, if he's looking at me.

"Okey dokey," I say, settling for the back of his neck as he bends over his shoelaces.

I go to the kitchen door and I already have a pretext ready. I'll go in for a glass of water.

I grab the handle, turn it, and *niente*, nothing. They'd locked it from the inside. Now it seems that you can't even pour yourself a glass of water.

"Papi, let me in," I whisper through the keyhole without knocking on the door.

I can sense him approaching.

"What does he want?"

"A glass of water, Papi."

I hear him breathing heavily. The old man must be having a hard time putting up with himself with this attitude he's got.

I imagine him with his ear glued to the keyhole and Mami in the background chewing on her nails.

"Glass of water my ass, what are you talking about, *figlio*! You're coming in here with your little errands, you come with your little messages!"

I try the door handle again.

"Open the door, Papi."

"I'm going to give him a message."

I tug on the handle and rattle the door.

"Tell your brother he's a traitor."

"Open the door, old man. I want to drink a glass of water."

The old lady must be wringing out a dishcloth or scratching her cheeks. She scratches her cheeks like a freak every time she feels sorry for herself.

Now my old man must have lit a cigarette.

"Tell him he's a reactionary."

"Okay, Papi. Now open the door."

"Tell him he doesn't understand anything. That this is his home. Tell him that I didn't send him to a university for five years so that he would go off to change himself on who knows what fucking island!"

My cigarette is burning down. With my mouth glued to the door, I drag the last of it down to the filter.

Now he's shaking the door as if he were rattling my neck.

"You tell your brother that he's no son of mine! Say it like that, nothing else. Tell him to get out of here."

I'll be fucked, I don't have another cigarette handy.

"Papi," I tell him, "give him a hug and let him go. You and I are revolutionaries, Papi. There's no point getting worked up about it."

He wiggles the door again, and this time more enthusiastically. I stand back a little, just in case.

"Nothing about you is revolutionary! You're just a fucking pothead! Tell your brother that I didn't pay for him to go to school for five years..."

"I know, old man."

"...five years at the university for him to go and work in I don't know what kind of shitty gas station in Australia. Tell him..."

Now *I* pound my fists on the door.

"Don't fuck around, old man!" I tell him.

I take advantage of the silence to light my last joint.

"Just shake his hand and that's it. If you don't you're going to be stuck with this old bullet in your side for the rest of your life. Tell *the old lady* to open the door. He asked me to tell you both. Your son wants to see you, Papi. Just shake his hand, it's not a big deal, Papi."

I try to listen, my eyebrows raised, to use my nose to figure out what's going on in there. My mother opening and closing the latch, uselessly filling glasses of water that she will raise to her mouth and spill without drinking them.

"For fuck's sake!" I say, and walk down the hall-way to my bedroom.

I find them on top of my bed, kissing. From her hair, in the way her hair was falling, I know they are kissing differently. She was accompanying her kiss with her hand on his hair, he was putting his hand under her arm, he was searching for the tip of her ear with his tongue. I have a feeling they should be making out with a team of translators.

I think: If he got her pregnant, who would react? La Paula was as new as new the first time she came to my room. She walked in wearing long college-girl stockings and a plaid miniskirt. La Paulita came to my room with my brother and I went to the movies just like one of those jerkoff kids who are the butt of some joke. I think that la Paula was with my brother because of that stupid thing that silly, timid chicks have for the assholes like my brother who drug them with their bla-bla-bla. I don't know how there are still hot chicks who sleep with guys who buy suits at Juvens and spend half the day smoking in front of the mirror.

Plus she's crying. Her green eyes have a slow lightning flash behind them, as if it were rising up from under some deep water. My brother must have gone over to console her and then started feeling her up. When he sees me he stands quickly and walks over to get a cigarette. He hands me the pack and doesn't look at me when he lights one. I'm also kind of hung up watching Paula wipe her face with the back of her hand, biting the back of it.

"What did they say to you?"

"They don't want to see you."

"Fucking parents."

We both suck on our cigarettes. He fixes the wave of hair on his head with his hand. He goes over to the lamp next to my bed and turns it on. So he can see the time.

"We'll have to get going."

My brother puts on his hat and slowly whistles a song that I've also heard on the radio, but I can't remember who sings it. Then he pats his back pocket. He checks to make sure the dollars he put together for his trip are still there. He says he's going to start out driving trucks, and then he'll get work in a gas station.

"Go talk to our parents," he says. "Tell them I'm leaving."

"They don't want to see you, asshole. They don't want to see you."

He scratches his neck.

"The old man's a dogmatist," he says, moving toward his jacket.

I tell him:

"Enough with the bullshit."

He turns around and this time he's really looking at me. He looks at me as if he's seen an animal coming into the room. A cat, I think.

"Might be better if you go talk to the old man."

I put my hands in my pockets and walk to the blinds. I close them and then open them again. Just out front, the lights come on. The green light on the wet sidewalk is like a sign of something. And the red glow from the traffic light. I tie a knot on the string that raises the blinds. My feet feel cold, and Paula is on the bed, spread out like a blanket. My brother kneels down, strokes her hair, and kisses her on the lips. Now that I look at him, I notice he has put on his jacket. He grabs one of the suitcases and points to the other one. I heave it up.

"It doesn't seem to be raining anymore," he says.

Now, with the broad suitcases tangled between our legs, the hallway seems much narrower. I walk hunched over, holding the suitcase out in front of me. My brother follows me with his hat on and his wavy hair falling down the middle of his nose. The space becomes wider in the entryway. There's a coatrack and a mirror. My brother moves forward and pulls out a comb with the same sudden speed a gangster reflects the light off the knife in his hand. He slowly tames his pompadour. He raises an eyebrow and turns in profile, and he tilts his head even more to see how his hair hangs down his back. He quickly shakes out the comb and puts it in the handkerchief pocket of his coat. I have no idea where this other cigarette I have between my fingers with the chewed tobacco flecks and a red film on the tip came from. I situate the two suitcases next to the door, the way we used to organize our toy army figures in symmetric rows when we were kids. Suddenly it occurs to me that we're still kids. That all of this is just a game. That Paula isn't Paula but Chabela, the maid's daughter. It occurs to me that this is just a game. That my brother will go for a walk around the block, come back with his mop of hair all tangled up and his cheeks scratched up and say: I was in Africa.

Finally, he puts on his white raincoat and, holding the lapels between his fingertips, he taps them lightly to adjust them. All this in front of the mirror. Then he turns around to speak to me. His body, his tweed suit, his Flaño perfume, his James Bond raincoat, his Sinatra hat, his Italian tie, his Yamil hairstyle, all of him turns around.

But even though he's dressed to the nines, his voice comes out all nasally and snotty like after a fight or a soccer match.

"Talk to them," he begs me.

I take another puff and knock on the kitchen door right there, next to the door to the street.

"Papá," I say, standing absurdly on my tiptoes, my mouth glued to the keyhole, which was giving off a thin light. "Papá, your son's right here. He wants to say goodbye."

Where I put my mouth before, I put my ear now. My eyes are fixed on my brother's eyes, which are looking up, his neck tense, as if he wanted to hear what's going on in there with his neck but not with his ears.

"Papá," I repeat, spurred on by one of my brother's gestures, "stop asking questions and talk to him. What's the big deal!"

He also walks up to the keyhole. At first we hear a murmur of voices. Mamá with her held-in-scream and he's mumbling.

My brother knocks on the door, looking straight ahead, as if he were going to walk through it. He has already raised his determined nose, a nose that is always in front of him, proud as a spear, demanding space. Those noses that you see on the posh people having their aperitifs in the Orient or waiting at an intersection in their Mercedes-Benz for the light to turn green.

I think: the old man's going to open the door for him.

I think: the old man's going to open this door and let out all of his rage with a knife in his hand.

Maybe all this shit is some kind of coincidence, a trick.

I think that maybe someone made a mistake when they allocated children to parents.

"Papá," my brother says.

His voice softens. He whispers, pressing the button on another machine. He doesn't want to leave home seething with rage; he doesn't accept that he has nothing left dripping inside his insolent skeleton.

"Papá," he says. "So long."

And he takes a step back, as if this movement were the distance agreed upon by some theater director. The silence between him and the door is like a wild animal. There's light from the kitchen suddenly and it spills out like an embrace. I remember those paintings with the apostles where a beam of light falling from heaven shines directly onto their foreheads. For a second he looks pale. For that brief second his nostrils have flared and his shoulders droop and a slight paunch reveals itself on his waist.

Papá appears in the foyer, his shirt open with the collar folded down, his hair graying and his eyes wet and dark. Mamá comes out from behind him with a kitchen towel twisted up in one hand.

"Are you leaving already, *figlio*?" he says.

My brother nods. Then he lowers his head and looks at the suitcases.

"Let me hug you, old man."

Mamá touches my father's back and it's the same thing as pushing him forward.

He rubs his right eyelid and stretches his short, hairy arms out in front of him. He grabs my brother and squeezes him as if he were going to bite him, and loosens his grip a little, and kisses him on the cheek, and then squeezes him again with his eyes closed. My brother reaches both arms under his armpits and up to his head and doesn't let go and buries the fingers on both his hands between his gray hair, and presses him closer to his face.

"I hope everything goes well, *figlio*," Papi says. My brother doesn't drag it out.

"Thanks," he says. And I can hardly hear him.

I think: let him go! but instead of moving toward them I back into the corner and lean against the wall.

The two detach themselves without looking at each other. Mamá steps forward, grabs him by the head, and shoves it into the hollow of her shoulder, wedging it between her shoulder and jaw, and he sighs with his eyes closed and his hands shake above her head as if they were sick.

When she loosens her embrace, my brother grabs a suitcase without looking at anyone and for me it's like I've been given an order and I pick up the other one and open the door for him so he can leave. And we go down the steps and we're already on the street and the lights skid over the pavement like slashing knives. Where did this cigarette I'm lighting right now come from? The cars pass by slowly and don't manage to lift the little bit of water that has been falling since morning. My brother pats his back pocket and walks to the curb, scrunching up his eyes and leaning out to see if he can spot a cab. With the tip of one finger, he lifts the cuff of his left sleeve and checks his watch. He puffs out his mouth and then tightens it, worried.

The Chevrolet coming down the middle of the road crosses cautiously toward the curb. We have to run a little because the car stopped farther ahead of us. My brother lowers his head into the window and explains that he's going to the airport. First he puts his suitcase on the front seat, and then he asks me for the one I'm holding, his hands shaking. I give it to him and he tosses it haphazardly into the back seat. There is a line of cars waiting behind us. It's strange that they don't honk their horns. Stranger still is that the silence has grown as the night approaches, as if the whole street were full of dead birds.

My brother comes toward me and from under his raincoat his two long, fast arms spring out and he looks me in the eyes and asks to wrap me in a hug.

But I look into his eyes and crouch down.

I look into his eyes and feel my neck sagging, my teeth gleaming.

Something stops my brother then.

He stands there for a moment with his hands empty and ambitious, his arms full of air, like a wind-mill without wind, like a ship without water.

At last he lowers his arms, smiles a little, sideways, and his nose gets sharper, more sharply outlined as it rises against the backdrop of the buildings. He's still smiling when he closes the door from inside the car. You can almost see the smile on the nape of his neck as the cab pulls away showing me the back of his head.

The kitchen door is ajar and my folks are drinking water in silence. I leak down the hallway until I reach my room. I don't know what's going on today that everything is so full of silence, I can't even think of a song to hum. Paula's body moves slowly at the back of the shadows. She raises her hand to her forehead to greet me and I walk over to the lamp and turn it off. Then I turn it on, and stand there scraping my lower lip with my teeth. I feel like clearing my throat, but I know how clearing my throat will sound and instead swallow my saliva slowly. I reach for a book on the shelf. I leaf through it without looking at it.

I think: when I grow up I'm going to know what to say in these situations; I'm going to have a mouth full of words; I'll stop crouching like a cat, pawing through books and shadows.

But I speak. Like a timid asshole my lips are moving.

"I have to study," my mouth says. "The exam's tomorrow."

Paula says:

"Sorry."

She gets off the bed. She straightens her hair, adjusts her skirt by sinking her fingers into her waistband. She picks up her raincoat. Grabs her purse.

I move over to her, take her by the arm, and stop her from walking toward the door.

"Don't go," I tell her. "You don't have to leave. I can study later. I can even not study if I feel like it." I said it and sounded like an idiot. Just to say something.

"All the same."

She swings her purse and I feel it flitting past my thigh over and over.

"Don't go!"

I walk over to her and arch my back to receive her. Her body falls into my embrace slowly and immediately I push her away to look at her. And her eyes are sweet and her mouth tired, and her cheeks burn under my fingertips. I kiss her hair, then her eyes. I kiss her on the mouth. And I hold her tight again. And she doesn't say anything. And she kisses me. And her tongue emerges from her mouth wet and fast and she caresses my neck with it and then she puts it back inside my mouth.

I pull her toward the bed, and we lie in each other's arms and press our heads together firmly, and each time we let go it's just so we can kiss. And we hold each other tight and let go and she doesn't say anything and I open her blouse and I don't know what to say to her and she doesn't know what to say to me and now we just hold each other. And I have this feeling that we are searching for each other's throats with our tongues.

"You're full of shit," I say to my brother.

fish

Wednesday morning at five o'clock
As the day begins.

THE BEATLES

When Grandma tripped in the kitchen and the china sugar bowl splintered on the floor and the little pieces were scattered all about, my mother, who was toasting breakfast bread over the gas stove, turned off the burner. She put her hands on her hips and, clenching her jaw, she whistled:

"For God's sake, Mamá!"

The old woman snorted but no words came out of her mouth. It was as if the remnants of an asthma attack were rattling around inside her. I knew that

Grandma had sharp teeth in her ears that juicily gnashed the words spoken to her and then, as if in response, she hacked them back out in generous gobs of spittle onto the dirt courtyard, attracting the attention of the pecking chickens.

I knew above all else that her asthma was an ocean that rose in her stomach when her daughter-in-law would call her "Mamá." The truth was, during the last minutes they had deadlocked and were having at each other through their underhanded insults. I nibbled with raised eyebrows on the crust of a stale *marraqueta*.

As she gathered all the debris together with her eyes, Mamá seemed to be building up stockpiles of rage. That was my *mamá*. Her engine overheated little by little. You could never tell how low she might go when her engine got hot.

She nudged the sugar bowl handle, which had come off almost entirely, with one of her feet and bent down to pick it up.

"Why don't you go to your room, Mamá?" she said.

I saw the old woman's glasses, held at the back of her neck by a black elastic band, jostling about. I made a broad bite into the bread and started to chew

it, kneading it around in my mouth, my eyes wide
open.

"Go to your room, Mamá! I'll bring breakfast to
both you and Nono," which is what she called my
grandfather.

Mamá was picking up the pieces one at a time,
and Grandma shared her opinion on the matter:

"It's better to brush it up with the broom."

Her Yugoslavian *r*'s trailed softly behind her. She
grabbed the broom from behind the door and tried to
start sweeping. Mamá got off the floor and snatched
the broom from her hands without looking at her.

"How can you think of sweeping when I'm pre-
paring breakfast?" she said. "Honestly, Mamá, you're
driving me..."

And her hands twitched and jerked on both sides
of her head as if a bolt of electricity had been shot at
her.

I dug a couple of fingers into the *marraqueta* and
pulled out a doughy mass of crumbs. The old woman
began to shake her head. She was in her seventies, but
you never really know how old grandmothers are.

"You are in your house," the old woman said.

She went to the sink, opened the faucet, and let the
water run.

"Mamá," my mother said. "What are you doing?"

"You are in your own house," my grandmother repeated.

She was grabbing and shifting all the glasses that were in the sink as if sorting through pieces of a jigsaw puzzle.

Mamá looked at her and I saw that vein in her throat start to bulge.

"What are you doing, *señora*?" she said.

"I had my own house," my grandmother said. "We were quiet and happy old people in my house."

She grabbed the kettle and put it under the faucet. She trampled on pieces of the broken sugar bowl with those fat legs of hers covered in bandages under her dark stockings.

"I'm not young anymore. I'm not healthy," she said. She turned off the water faucet and carried the kettle over to the gas stove.

"Mamá, go to your room," my mother said. "I'll make breakfast for you."

The old woman tried to grab the box of matches, but she was too nervous. The toothpicks spilled all over the floor. I looked through the sunny window onto the patio and put my hand on the window latch, thinking about going to lie down on the beach chair.

"How much longer will you keep fucking things up, señora," my mother said.

"How much longer will you keep fucking things up," she repeated, emphasizing each word.

I saw her stare at my mother with her blue gaze. Her wrinkled white skin couldn't quite hold on to the rage she seemed to have.

"This old woman isn't going to be fucking things up anymore," she said, moving toward the hallway. "I'll leave with my old man right now."

I used the toe of my shoe to hide some of the broken pieces under the cupboard. Mamá followed her out of the kitchen, and shouted toward her room:

"Do whatever you want, *s'ñora!*"

She came back into to the kitchen. After breaking the first match, she managed to light the second one and put the kettle on to boil. Papá appeared in the doorway wearing just his T-shirt. He was freshly shaved and there was still a little shaving cream under his ears. He was holding his shirt in his hand and his white muscles bulged the short sleeves of his T-shirt.

"What's going on?" he asked curtly, looking at me but obviously asking Mamá.

"What do you think?" my mother exclaimed without looking at him. "Grandma again."

Papá looked at me for a while longer and then his eyes lingered on the burner. He ran his hand across his chin, verifying the effectiveness of his shave. I dug my fingers back into the bread and pulled a thick mass of crumbs from it.

"She fucks about, fucks up, and fucks with my head!" Mamá added, her voice guarded, though she was actually shouting it.

Papá raised his eyebrows.

"Well," he said.

We could hear the old woman's vague grunts in the silence. She seemed to be moving the furniture around. I heard Grandpa talking. "Shit," I heard him say. And I didn't hear the rest, but I could guess. Whenever he said "shit," he added "Yankee, syphilitic, fantastic." At the end he said, "chicken fucked in the ass." When the old man still had his legs he'd go out to the courtyard and feed the laying hens, which was when the young chickens loose in the yard were brought into the coop to peck their grain. Then he'd kick at them and tell them what I just said. He had no affection for chickens. He wasn't fond of Yankees either.

The truth is that one time he overdid it and cleated a chicken and opened it up and its guts bubbled out and everything. Grandma grabbed the dying bird and, stuffing its guts in, sewed the skin back up with black thread. Then she said that phrase to Grandpa that he wished he'd never heard. She told him: "God is going to punish you for kicking chickens' asses." I say that because later Grandpa got gangrene and they cut off one of his legs. And then they cut the other one off. They cut the other one off two months later. And now Nono is an old man in his wheelchair and he watches every program on TV and sometimes I take him for a walk along Costanera and we talk about horses.

As for the chicken, we ate it months later, cooked in the oven. Grandma said: "This is the chicken the old man kicked."

Just now Grandma entered the kitchen; her silence was solemn. She went to the sideboard and took out two large Czechoslovakian china plates that she'd had since the day she was married. She also took out two forks and two knives. She took out two spoons. Then she turned around and went back to her bedroom.

"What's she doing?" Papá asked, leaning against the refrigerator.

"She says she's leaving," my mother replied, flinging her arms into the air.

"What did you say to her?"

"What do you want me to say to her? She said she's leaving. She broke the sugar bowl."

I walked down the hallway and stood there caressing my piece of bread. Papá peeked through the old folks' bedroom door and stood under the door lintel. Grandpa was disheveled, his hair white and flowing, waiting for breakfast with the empty tray resting on the sheets.

Papá continued to study his shave, tracing the corner of his right lip with his fingers. I stood beside him and we took in all the hustle and bustle.

Grandma had opened the trunk, and she tossed Nono's blue pinstriped suit onto the bed. I had seen that wardrobe opened on Sundays, when Grandma would take out her rosary, her black tulle, and her wide lace dress. But today was Friday and she put Grandpa's suit on the bed. It was a suit that also came out only on Sundays, but two years ago. I mean it's a suit with pant legs and everything. Grandpa used to get dressed up to go to the races and he wore that suit. "Príncipe," the old woman would call him as the old man put on his suit and walked slowly down the main street searching for the bus to the racetrack. That's what I remembered, leaning there against the doorframe next to my father. I also remembered Juan Rivera winning a close photo decision and that we went to play bocce at Turco's and my grandfather had made a lot of money from Juan's horse and we bought a roast suckling pig and a carafe and ate it that night at home, before my grandfather moved to this house, which is my parents' house, and the warehouse went to hell.

"The disease," the old man said, wiping a green, insolent tear down the wall of his hooked nose.

"The asses," the old woman would say, looking at you over the glasses she wore for knitting.

Nono swallowed hard, his hands on the blanket, and he clicked his tongue worriedly, looking toward the window. Grandma said something to him in Yugoslavian, and the old man clicked his tongue again and kept looking at the window.

My father dug into his ear with a finger.

"Can you tell me what you're doing, Mamá?"

The old woman kept on emptying the wardrobe. Her dressing gown had appeared. I liked the way that gown smelled. It smelled both old and good. Sometimes I thought about what amazing boobs Grandma must have had when she was young.

"We're leaving, *mijito*," she said, wiping the first beads of sweat from her forehead. My *nona* was sweet and fat. Also pale. Fat and pale. My grandfather, on the other hand, was skinny and pale. The sun never touched them, and sometimes, if I forgot Grandpa for a while in the yard when I got distracted reading, the fuzz on his face would frizz, and then he'd look in the mirror and pull out those little scorched hairs.

The thing is that you can't even touch old people with a flower petal.

My *papá* had been getting really excited about his finger in his ear.

"Where are you going, Mamá?"

"We're going to look for a room."

Papá nodded and I felt like he was looking at me sideways.

"In which boardinghouse, Mamá?"

"I'll know when I see it, son. As long as I can work." Papá cleared his throat, but he didn't move.

"There aren't any boardinghouses around here. You'll have to go downtown. If that's the case, he won't be able to get on the bus in his wheelchair."

Grandma moved closer to Nono so she could take off his pajamas. The old man looked out the window haughtily. Now that it was a little later, the sunlight was creeping across the quilt. Just by looking at it I felt the bed getting warm.

"Did you hear what I said, Mamá?"

She was putting on his shirt, a nice shirt with
a frilly collar and narrow blue stripes on the white
fabric. The truth was that Grandpa had grown gaunt
and he was drowning in his shirt. He had the face of a
surprised bird.

"We're going to walk there, my boy. As long as
Nona has her legs..."

Papá turned his back on her and walked to the
dining room. Now I realized that breakfast was ready
because the toast was giving off a lovely aroma and
Mamá would be putting butter on it. Of course,
Mamá didn't say anything. Today we had to guess
that breakfast was ready.

They had already opened the curtains, and the red
checkered tablecloth with the full breadbasket, steaming coffee, and jam looked nice. I sat in the middle
seat across from my mother, with my back to the hallway that connected to the bedrooms. Papá scratched
hard on his scalp and both he and my mother gri-
maced and sighed. I put a piece of crusty bread in
my mouth and watched them chewing quietly. Papá
would moisten the *marraqueta* in his café con leche, let
it drip into the cup, and then suck on it while looking
out the window. But he was looking in a very peculiar

way. As if he were on the moon. Mamá was also out
if it, but instead of looking out the window she was
clinking her spoon in her coffee cup.

So much stirring, I thought, if she drinks it without
sugar.

A little while passed, more or less. In the meantime I memorized all the stains on the tablecloth. We
grabbed the sugar bowl and put it next to the teapot.
We grabbed the teapot and placed it next to the milk;
we took the lid off the sugar bowl. Papá whistled a
marching tune, the one from *The Bridge on the River
Kwai*, and my mother finger-curled her hair with her
head resting on one hand. What fascinated me was
the replacement sugar bowl. It had fat blue angels on
the pink porcelain stoneware. Precisely the sugar bowl
we use on Sundays. Everything was arranged as if we
were expecting visitors.

Suddenly a noise in the hallway, the unmistakable, creaking, and squeaky sound of the poorly oiled
wheelchair, drew my father's attention to his right. I,
who had my back to them, twisted my neck, and then,
leaning on the corner of the table, I turned my whole
body. Papá sipped from his cup, not looking at it, waiting for the door to open.

And sure enough, the door opened.

But Grandma didn't appear. It was Grandpa who appeared, wedged into his wheelchair, rolling toward the front door. The vehicle came to a stop well before it crashed into it. Right in the middle of the living room.

I now turned the whole chair around and looked at Grandpa in his entirety. A wide blue necktie had been tied around the collar of his striped shirt. Smooth. And over that, his suit jacket, mannish and a little dirty. As for the pants, Grandma's practical hand was visible. She had folded the excess under the chair cushion. Which was everything from a little above the knees, more or less. But what made my eyes flit over Grandpa's head, as if I were a bird hovering over a nest, was the impeccable short-brimmed hat that had been planted on his disheveled brow. I had lusted after that hat in my furtive incursions into my grandparents' closet, under its nylon dust cover. But I had also removed it once and stuck my whole hand inside, fingering the label with my curious fingers. "Stetson, London," it said. Now, under that outlined blackness, his nose stood out abruptly, pale. And stuffed up.

Only once did he glance at us during the long while the old woman left his chair stuck in the center of the room almost like a dagger stabbed into wood, like a sack of spilled oranges. He looked at us with his watery green eyes, but he didn't touch us with his gaze. He looked at us mutely, if it can be said like that. Without touching each other with our glances. As if some wind had torqued his neck in our direction. And immediately (I say immediately but that's wrong, it happened all at once, fast and unnoticed) he put one hand over the other, the two bony ones calm and useless, and spilled his eyes over the courtyard.

I looked at Mamá.

When she noticed my gaze and looked at me, I grabbed the butter dish, stuck the knife in it, and started scraping some butter over my toast.

Papá had put his shirt on and was now unbuttoning his sleeves almost professionally.

I remembered, while I was spreading the icy butter on the already cold bread, my friends in the neighborhood. I thought of them, when we used to exchange comic books and I would park the old man in the shade of a kiosk until I finished reading them. And also the day when I left a couple of magazines on the chair, and when I came back I found the old man laughing at the drawings. Mostly I remembered what they used to say to me when I took Grandpa out for a walk. They'd say: "Your little baby girl is so cute."

And of course, Nono was a tiny piece of a grandpa without his legs. With his little gaze, his cute, toothless smile. And his eyes limp, but comfortable. Like a mirror.

When the old woman appeared, she was carrying a small suitcase and a basket: a frying pan, a soup ladle, and a large jar of Colman's English mustard were sticking out of it. The silver crucifix that they hung above their headboard, the Bible, and their rosaries were also visible. She moved more and more slowly, and the whistling noise in her chest became more constricted. Her glasses, tethered by that black elastic, hung across her chest.

"Here," she said to Grandpa, handing him the suitcase.

She immediately balanced it on the old man's knees, and when she had rigged a solid platform, she placed the basket on top of it.

If I hadn't had him in profile, I would have lost sight of Grandpa altogether. The ladle covered his nose, and the handle of the basket floated above his little black hat. It looked like a shopping cart, that wheelchair. I imagined that Nono, the way he was going now, wouldn't be able to see the landscape. Just as well, I thought immediately, that the basket is going to keep the sun out of his face. They were going to have the sun in their eyes and overhead because the cheap boardinghouses were in the heart of the city. And Grandma wouldn't have much money in her black crocheted bag.

Papá approached Grandpa, and he pushed the ladle away from his nose, to the left side.

"How are you doing, Nono?" he said.

He called him "Nono," but he is his *papá*. Just because I exist, everyone calls Grandpa Nono. He was a big-time racehorse gambler and he still enjoys fiddling with the odds on Sunday mornings. Now my *papá* calls his own father Nono.

The old man sat still like a picture. As if he'd been painted all of a sudden. Papá lifted his hat a little and used his breakfast napkin to wipe away some black line and a bit of dirt that had left their mark on his forehead.

"Where are you two going, Nono?" he asked.

"Syphilitic, fantastic," Grandpa said.

My mother approached the chair at the precise moment that Grandma, swimming in her wide black dress, appeared in the doorway and walked over to the old man to take hold of the wheelchair handles. Whenever that happened, Grandpa would shift his weight a little to the front and flip the latch lever himself. I would have wanted to help, but it occurred to me that if I opened the door for them, it would give the impression that I was complicit in something.

So I stayed where I was, stirring the coffee dregs with my spoon.

The old woman had to go over and open the door herself. When she came back she looked at us without any real purpose, almost as if she was really our guest, a visitor who had her own house, garden, and telephone, who had been invited over for breakfast and was now returning to her luxurious routine.

At the door she seemed to be chewing on a phrase. Maybe one of those you say at the end of a party. One of those rhyming and surprising verses that end all the best patriotic poems. Or one of those by Amado Nervo. We got quieter and quieter, and we squeezed and squeezed and squeezed the silence.

The five of us looked like a forest at night, no breeze and all the birds asleep. It seemed like the screeching wheels going through the yard were like a slow, jagged dagger sawing through a piece of flesh, a dagger sliding across the stomach.

When it was just the three of us, I noticed that Papá had put his tie on. I noticed that Mamá was crying, although she wasn't making any noise. My father grabbed *El Mercurio* and started to leaf through the pages above the remnants of his breakfast. Mamá pulled a flannel rag out of her apron and started wiping up the crumbs.

Like someone who wants nothing to do with what's going on, I went into the front yard and put a matchstick between my teeth. Our house was on one of those steep streets, and you had to walk up the incline to get to the center of town. So I sat down on a street step and from there I watched the old woman's broad back creep up the hill and blend into the edges of the chair. The two of them looked like a single animal. An old, ringworm-ridden donkey, its hair falling out like silly signs no one paid any attention to. I remembered the story of Tom Thumb, when the dipshit is throwing out the bread crumbs and the birds come and eat them. I don't know why, but as my *nonos* reached the corner, it seemed to me that they were falling apart, that the sun was making them vibrate with some kind of dark electricity that was making their skin even more wrinkly, and as the old woman dried the sweat on her forehead her face was being erased, and that the black Stetson hat was devouring Grandpa. I thought I could see his worn-out, distant green eyes.

When they disappeared, I tied the laces of my basketball shoes and started to run up the hill. After a few meters I felt like the sun was beating down on me; I was panting. It felt like an unpleasant, dirty tickle. It didn't take me long to get to the corner. The cross street was flat, full of oil stains and discrete potholes. Cracks that the sun had made in the old concrete. From that moment on, I followed the old couple from half a block back, like those dogs that follow the peanut vendors, the vegetable wagons, wagging their tails.

I saw them in the middle of the white sun's violent flickering, which was inflicted on my eyes and spilled like glistening milk on the sidewalks. I watched them wobble toward a corner that was always a little farther away. I saw them on the sticky asphalt, their wheels and legs slipping forward, exhausted. The city was full of green wooden houses with coffee-colored trim. The houses were painted green because there were no trees. The scant side yard plants sprouted up because someone had peed there, or sweet old ladies watered them with rusty peach jars. But they were skinny plants that gave no shade. Someday I'll up and leave this town. I'll travel south and eat melon-flavored ice cream under a broad tree. In my head those trees looked like bulls. I didn't see any animals here. The termites that drilled into the wood of the warehouses. Rats.

Give me a break, rats and termites animals! Cats, animals!

I saw the old couple turn the corner and I had to run so I wouldn't lose sight of them for even a second. Now they were going more slowly. It seemed like they were wilting in the clear, thick air. Even though it was early morning, the sun was pounding down, not life-giving but withering. Like if you put a kettle on the fire but there's no water and the kettle becomes a worthless glob of shit. I felt like letting my grandparents wither away on their own. Let them become a single mass of old black molasses giving themselves over to the empty streets. I could go to the public swimming pool. Swim to the raft, play with the neighborhood girls and dunk them under the water and dive with them and grab them by the waist and rub their breasts, and get it on with them a little on the boulders.

I saw the old folks lose momentum, like an enormous spinning top beginning to wobble and bobble and tilt. Just like a drunk falling next to a lamppost slowly, proudly, with his mug drooping open. I saw them flatten out on the sidewalk. The old lady was no longer pushing the cart; she had lain down on the cart. I saw her inside the cart! Unless, I said. And I crossed the sidewalk to get a better look at their profiles.

Right beside the walls in front of them, that's when I saw what the old man was doing.

I saw that my grandma was sort of fainting, all her girth on the chair, and the old man was pushing the wheels with both hands, as if the chair was a boat, a heavy boat, and he was rowing it. And his arms would go backward and you could make out his elbows through his swelling jacket.

Sweet old woman, I thought. To the bitter end, old hag. She wants the old man to rupture his liver dressed like a black prince, like a dark angel.

I saw the old couple in a knot, in a ball, tottering along. Maybe foaming at the mouth, how could I know! Oh the old couple a black cloud a sad and big bird wallowing in the dirt of the inflexible city! Oh the old folks a sickly cloud expelled from the galaxy brought down to be pissed on by dogs and cats and termites and rats!

My heart was a tightly clasped fist, pounding. So bang bang fuck fuck fuck and shit shit shit I was being pulled back and forth, crouching like I was in some kind of dance.

I saw the old man, his arms looked like skinny, throbbing spears, he looked like a worn-out train engine, I saw him without his two legs but with his heart clinging, enduring those blows his arms were inflicting upon him. All at once I saw, on the edge of the dusty wall, a galley of slaves in the hold of the ship with their veins throbbing in their muscles, and above them, like pompous birds, the English captains, young, with their indifferent noses, protecting themselves with their handkerchiefs from a light foam that the wind was tempering onto the deck. And down below the rowers, dirty, with flies biting their necks. The city was the tail end of a sand dune and the old man's elbows were lagging behind. The city a wasteland. Like this constellation. Just like a bad dream on a Sunday afternoon, a nightmare under the sun at four o'clock in the afternoon. The old man was spinning his wheels now in the same place. He'd found a door he couldn't get through. The still, uninhabited space paralyzed him, his face like a bird crashing to the ground. I thought: this is their home.

I thought they will fall asleep there, in the white, unpopulated street, and the sun will fall in vertical rays upon them, the sun will suck them dry like a hot sponge.

Then they weren't moving.

The truth is that there were buses passing by, and now that I think about it, there are people in the vestibules, shopkeepers with black briefcases and dazzling ties, copper-colored employees, young mothers with their tits out and their babies grumbling at them. And among them, the old couple dead like a tree. Just like an insignificant river that had dried up and the last drop was absorbed by a rotten pebble, pure and simple.

The old couple lingered there, painted in a bad picture, the shoulder of the asthmatic old woman convulsing, the sweet-eyed old man petrified on the sidewalk.

I approached them with my hands in the pockets of my blue jeans and stood beside them, watching their breasts expand and contract like wounded lungs, the old woman's springy, wide, feathery, scattered, and desperate. The old man's electric and pale. They looked at me looking at them, unsurprised, almost distracted. The old woman raised her bent back slightly and dug her chubby fingers around the bar to push the chair. Nono moved his hands away from his chest and crossed them over the pan that was sticking out of the basket, lifting them up. Ten meters away there was a bus stop, and we went over to it so we could pant in the shade. And we stood there sluggishly until their bodies become more concentrated. We spent about half an hour watching people pass by, looking after them as their shadows widened behind them. I also watched the buses leave and a strange thing happened. High up on the lamppost, the shadows of the buses passed in front of us and then quickly spilled out like black water. And my *nonos* were also a shadow. But a lead shadow. Like the essence of something. And I looked at my shadow, too. And it looked like a tree.

Suddenly the old man spoke.

"I'm hungry," he said.

Nona came up to me and wiped the sweat off her eyelids with her handkerchief. Her forehead was dry.

Grandma looked at me and pushed the cart easily.

"Let's go," she said.

At the corner I realized that they were going to lap the block. As soon as she turned the corner, she stopped in front of the fishmonger who sold fish from baskets with ice wrapped in sacks inside them. She caught a red conger eel by the tail and held it up to the sun looking for reflections. The beast looked beautiful. The owner weighed it on the portable scale and the old woman said to give it to her as it was, not to skin it, not to cut it up.

She told the owner that she wanted it in one piece.

He handed me the fish wrapped in the supplement from *El Mercurio*.

"Take it," he said.

Now we were making our way down the hill and Nona had to keep braking the cart. The pavement was bumpy on that stretch, and when a piece of gravel lifted the wheelchair, Grandpa nearly lost his hat. He finally caught it against his neck and put it back on. But he didn't put it on straight and wedged on his forehead like Grandma had arranged it earlier. It rested over his left ear and drooped a little over his forehead. And then he used a couple of his fingers and pretended he had a thick Toscano, and pretended to put it in his mouth, and pretended that he was blowing smoke rings. He looked at me, raising his eyebrows, and said:

"Humphrey Bogart."

And then he tipped off the ashes as if he were whacking a Ping-Pong ball and said:

"Yankee, syphilitic, fantastic."

It was much easier to get the chair into the living room than out of it. All we had to do was push the bar

downward for the chair to settle onto the step. Papá
had left for work and Mamá was cooking some rambunctious noodles over a low flame. The old man was
installed in the dining room, next to the bay windows,
and Nona came to join me in the kitchen.

"What have you got there, Mamá?" my mother
asked. The old woman unwrapped the conger eel and
shook it vigorously by the tail.

"I bought this conger eel from the fishmonger," she
said. "I'm going to boil it and cook it with the skin on."

"That's the way Nono likes it," my mother said.

I went out to the patio to read a comic book. It's
true that I like to linger around the kitchen and watch
what people are doing. I have a genuine passion for
watching people when they're working. But this time
I left, anxious to read the comics. I read *Barbarella*, an
old *Barrabases*, and skimmed through the horse listings
for Sunday.

I guess a while had passed, because when Grandma
called me I looked up and saw that none of the things
around me had a shadow. They were alone and lying
around.

I knew what I had to do. I went to the glass bureau
and pulled out the napkin in the shape of a bib. I went
up to Nono and hung it around his neck.

"The little baby," the old man said.

I tied it behind him and then turned around to see Grandma place the steaming plate on the Yugoslavian tray. Nono plunged his spoon in and gave a torrential blow over his first spoonful. He immediately opened his mouth and spooned it in, mashing it slowly. When he gulped it down, his lips opened long and horizontal and then he ran his tongue over his underpopulated gums. Then he stuck his tongue back in his mouth and smiled.

I went for a long walk around the neighborhood because I can't stand fish.

ballad for
a fat man

When Juan Carlos joined our class, we were all happy because we needed a fat guy, our own *gordo*.

He showed up in the middle of our English class and our smile was as quick and crass as a rat. We were familiar with the feminoid hysterics of Mr. Smith (Smith and an English teacher!) and we sensed that our laughter couldn't go beyond our diaphragms without it going unpunished: there it convulsed in our empty stomachs during that first hour of our morning class. If any laughter appeared on our faces it was a frown across the mouth or some insolent sparkle in our eyes.

Juan Carlos was accompanied by a small inspector, so thin he was insignificant, whose suits never covered his ankles or wrists. We decided that Inspector Soto bought his suits in the children's section of Falabella to save money. It was precisely Soto who pushed Juan Carlos into the room, offering him to Mr. Smith like a cow taken to a butcher. At one point they were each holding one of his arms and the *gordo* was smiling at them blankly, turning back and forth like a fan every time they spoke to him.

"Valparaiso," I heard him say suddenly.

From the back of the room I calculated that we would all be doing the math. Fifteen for Chile, ten for Colo-Colo, eight for Católica, two for Audax. If Gordo was for the Wanderers soccer club, he would practically be the official representative of the provinces and the Monday morning urinal discussions would take on an additional attraction. When Soto pointed to a bench in the middle row, we guessed that we'd have to turn our shoulders into the aisle so he'd be able to squeeze past us. He did it with a notebook in his hand and he wore that smile that made it seem like he was blushing at first and as the days passed we realized he was simply arrogant.

"I won the *gordo*, the lottery, the big money's coming my way," Dorfman, Blondie as we called him, whispered, his mouth watering as he watched the fat kid make his way forward.

Juan Carlos sat down and of course we all looked into the aisle to see how many centimeters of his butt cheek fell over the wood. Mr. Smith distracted our curiosity with his typical teacher attitude from a Yankee movie. He thought he was crazy Mr. Novak.

"*I want you to meet our new friend,*" he said in English, "*Mr. Juan Carlos Osorio. Say hello to him, people.*"

"*Hi,*" we exclaimed in a tone much shriller than our natural one.

"Juan Carlos," Mr. Smith said, "*do you want to tell your friends where you come from?*"

Dorfman jabbed Gordo with his elbow, telling him to stand up.

Juan Carlos stood up with his eyes run over by a bunch of loose eyelashes that blinked from the floor to Smith, from Smith to the blackboard, from the blackboard to Smith, from Smith to the floor.

"*I don't speak English,*" he muttered in a cavernous accent.

"*Beg your pardon?*" Mr. Smith projected, imitating the disparaging gesture of the old aristocrats in Alec Guinness movies.

He had walked over to the bench and with his neck craned he rummaged flirtatiously through the fat guy's notebook.

Juan Carlos was more spare the second time:

"*No English,*" he said.

Mr. Smith inserted his thumbs into the two small pockets on his vest and from there commanded the rest of his fingers to drum his chest.

"A Humanities sixth year and '*no English*'?" he said, mocking Juan Carlos's coarse diction. "*Why?*" he added in English but then switched back to Spanish. "Out of laziness, ignorance, disinterest?"

The fat kid looked at his forehead.

"As a matter of principle," he responded.

Mr. Smith twisted his neck slightly and waved his fingers as if fanning himself.

"*My soul,*" he exclaimed.

During the break between classes, Juan Carlos leaned against the second-floor railings, projecting his robust backside out into the hallway. He was looking placidly at the palm tree in the courtyard when I walked up to him, unwrapping the paper from my sandwich and offering him half of it.

"You want some, Osorio?"

He reached out an indifferent hand and took a piece of *marraqueta*. He opened it expertly with his thumb, like someone leafing through a book, and after closing it, he gave the crispy dough a generous chew.

"Call me 'Guatón,'" he said, and I looked at his broad paunch and thought that some nicknames fit us perfectly.

He finished the bread off with the second bite and kneading the morsel in his mouth he tapped his index finger on my chest repeatedly while gesturing that he was waiting to be free of the mouthful to talk to me.

"Call me 'Guatón,' that's all," he said finally.

At the end of that day we had an hour off and went down to the gym with the boys to play "baby-soccer." Juan Carlos came down the stairs chatting with a group, but instead of starting with a warm-up shot at the goal, he stretched out on the karate mat, held his face with his right hand, and then pulled out a book with a gray cover.

"What are you jerking off to, Guatón?" Hernán González asked him.

Gordo gave us a bored look and lifted the cover a little so we could catch the title.

"Ex-trem-ism-as-a-child-ish-dis-ease-by-the-rev-ol-u-tion-ar-y-Vlad-i-mir-Il-yich-Len-in," Hernán whistled flatly.

"Is it good?" I asked, switching the ball to my other hand.

Juan Carlos put all the fingers of his free hand together and shook them at us.

"Like this!" he said.

González glanced at the book again and immediately looked over Guatón's flabby body sprawled across the mat.

"Will you lend it to me later?"

"Sure," Guatón said. And added without looking up, "If you don't understand something, I'll explain it to you."

"Me too, Gordo," I said.

We gathered in the bathroom during the first break we had on Saturday to smoke cigarettes and frantically plan that night's party.

"Do you have any snacks?"

We dreaded the thought of spending the night listening to the radio or playing cards with our girl-friends' parents. We'd need to have a party anywhere we could. Many of us already had official girlfriends, and on Saturdays they had high-class tastes and smelled like babies who had wiped their asses with talcum powder. Everyone and their grandmother showered with their younger brother's cologne or showed up with Richmond cigarettes inside their jackets.

That morning we decided it would be Dorfman's sister's birthday party. Blondie called a little meeting in the last toilet stall so the news wouldn't spread and the class assholes wouldn't descend upon it like parachutists.

He picked González, Marcelo Charlín, Múttoli, Pije Marín, and Gilberto Llanos.

"Don't let the cat out of the bag," he warned.

Guatón was taking a piss behind me.

I nodded toward him with my chin and asked Dorfman with my eyes if we should invite him.

"Tell him," he said.

The last thing he said:

"Bring drinks."

"Gordo," I said, joined by my group, "we want to invite you to a party tonight."

Juan Carlos tucked his business inside his pants and pulled up his zipper.

"Whose house?"

"Dorfman's."

"Can I bring my girlfriend?"

I didn't see González's or Llanos's face, but I sensed the expressions of ironic amazement in their profiles. I knew what they were thinking because I was thinking the same thing. I knew they were thinking about Juan Carlos's girlfriend, what she'd be like. That is, I knew they were thinking about Saraghina in *8½*.

"I suppose so," I said, controlling the irony on my lips.

"Of course," Llanos said.

"Terrific," Gordo said.

And later: "I have something for you."

And he handed me a red hardcover book that turned out to be *The Communist Manifesto* by Marx and Engels.

He then lumbered down the bathroom hallway to the door, and there he turned to González.

"Read it, both of you," he said, pointing a finger at us, "and when you finish, I'll lend you another one."

He was about to disappear behind the door when he hesitated for a second.

"And if there's something you don't understand, ask, you hear me?"

I put the book under my arm and then faced the urinal because I almost pissed myself I was laughing so hard.

That night the news that Gordo was coming with his girlfriend had spread around half of Chile.

"Let's see if he brings her in a truck."

"Gentlemen, I'm quite lean…"

"He's going to need help getting her off the truck."

"When he gets here, anchor those canapés down."

I was categorically opposed to Múttoli playing a popular record that made fun of fat people on the record player. When I realized he had left it within reach for the triumphal entry, I slid the record under an armchair and it was never seen again.

Around ten that night, our shirt collars were dirty and our necks were a little dizzy. It wasn't time yet for what we called the *cheek to cheek* and since Skármeta was the disc jockey, we still hadn't gotten past the prehistory of Elvis Presley and Ricardito. About that time, a bunch of us went out to the porch to talk all kinds of bullshit. We were always together like that: a swig of Cuba libre, which was rum and Coke, whatever and Coke in one hand, and in the other a cigarette that we would stub out, looking sideways at the chicks, appraising their legs, sniffing their neck-lines, testing our footing for later when the lights would dim and González would manage to disconnect the overhead lamp.

That's what we were doing, smoking and smoking and drinking and drinking, when we saw Juan Carlos get out of a cab. We all spotted him at the same time. And at that very moment I knew why. I knew it was because we had gone out to the porch to wait for him. We had spotted him at the same time because we all wanted to be the first to see Gordo's girlfriend.

Múttoli went down the two steps and strode spell-bound through the yard. I walked to the column and crouched down with a crumpled cigarette between my teeth.

And then, just as Gordo finished, with a little diffi-culty, paying the cab fare she appeared. I didn't want to look at anyone's face. I simply felt how all the saliva that had gathered in my mouth was now sliding down my throat. We were like little boys just learning to masturbate. We were going out with meager-breasted, ponytailed chicks. Chicks with high waists and va-ginas closed up until that wedding ring was on their finger. We'd only seen females with verdant hips and breasts like apples in CinemaScope. At the Astor premieres, we hadn't seen them anymore after that.

And it's not that Gordo's girlfriend was a beauty, not even that her body was harmoniously pressed into her dress, maybe she was even too short for so much breast and so much wiggling on her haunches. But what was so irresistible, what was so fascinating, what was so unnerving about this female, was the savagely painted red mouth with its boisterous teeth and then her long, wet gaze.

Gordo sat down in the middle of the group, and, wiping his perspiration away with the back of his hand, he said to us:

"Allow me to introduce you to my girlfriend."

We held out our hands in mock indifference.

"It's a pleasure to meet you."

Two hours later Gordo and I were slumped over the table, arguing about who was going to win the '64 election. I must have consumed half a ton of Cuba libre, and I had to twist up my lips just to utter a monosyllable. Gordo talked and banged his fist on the tablecloth, and when he wasn't speaking because I had taken the floor, he would light his cigarette, which would go out every now and then. At one point I thought it was a nice, intimate, passionate conversation, but as I attempted to take another drink I noticed that we were actually arguing and that half the class was participating with their eyes wide open the way they do sometimes.

I don't remember what I said then, but I'm guessing. I mean, I can't hear anything anyone says to me when there's a record playing in the background. I remember that the record was "Love Me Do" by the Beatles, but I don't remember what it was that *I* was arguing about with Gordo. I do remember when Pije Marín told him from behind my back:

"You're fucking it up, Guatón. We still don't have the right to vote and you're already talking communist bullshit."

"What you mean is," Gordo said, "that we can't fight."

"We're too young," Marín said.

Guatón took out a picture. I clumsily rolled my neck around and looked at it and all I saw was a bunch of dead people. They looked like a family.

He shoved it in front of Marín's nose.

"Look at that, Pije, you snob," he said. "What do you see here?"

Marín gave it a quick glance and then a sly, disdainful look down his nose.

"A picture with some dead assholes."

"Do you know who they are?"

"They must be from the Vietnam War. You guys always bring up the same bullshit."

"You mean to say," I said, possibly standing up, "that you supported the Yankee war in Vietnam."

"Hold on." Gordo calmed me down.

He shoved the picture back in Marín's face. That crazy Múttoli was also standing next to him.

"This isn't Vietnam, Pije."

Marín shrugged his shoulders.

"This is Santiago. These people you see *here* were massacred by a right-wing government, *here* in Chile."

Pije adjusted the knot of his tie.

"It's unfortunate that these things happen," he said. "And besides that, I'm against the war in Vietnam."

Gordo tucked the photo under his vest.

"And now you still think we're too young to get involved in politics?"

Marín lit a cigarette.

"And these kids in the photo, weren't they too young to be killed?" Gordo accused with an imperious finger.

"Anyway," Pije said.

Gordo stared at him as if waiting for another word, but Pije looked away and pretended to reach for a bottle that was lying on the tablecloth. Then he looked around and when he saw that everyone else was so quiet, he said, "I'm going to the bathroom."

An hour later I was dancing with Francisca, my girlfriend that year, tight against her belly. Whenever I drank I always felt like doing the same thing with her. Then she arched back a little so as not to feel it between her legs and her ass was a little perky. At this point in the night I was starting to tell her that she was hot and that we should go to bed. That we were too old to be acting like the other stupid little horny couples. That we'd been dating for a year and what was up with that.

After these conversations, still nothing happened. Except that she'd start crying and I'd take her to a stairwell and would comfort her a little and I'd touch her tits a little, too. At that exact moment, the same thing was happening in every corner of the house.

There was more back-and-forth, more give-and-take between these couples than in a Turkish market. In short, little bastards that we were, we got our hands covered with hairspray from so much hair shaking and pulling and we drowned our crazy desire in alcohol, as the tangos used to say. The girls' makeup would get all messed up, their faces would get all hot, and of course they had to go to the bathroom for a couple of lustrums to tidy themselves up.

That's where I left my Francisquita, she was so beautiful I had to adjust the havoc she caused on me with my hands in my pockets as I walked through the second floor to the terrace and began to look at the moon. When I couldn't look at the moon any longer I began to walk around the terrace, relieved that my dick was calming down.

Basically, we were so young that we spent the whole day talking about fucking girls. There wasn't any more room on the benches for even one more ball sack. We'd started drawing them on the backrests of the benches. So, when I looked through the terrace window and saw what my eyes were seeing, I fell on my face and to the side, afraid that the noise my heart was making would enter the room. I leaned against the wall, stuck a little piece of my nose and this whole eye out toward the glass, and saw them pressed to the bed like a pin into paper.

Gordo was with his naked girlfriend on the blanket. Not completely. What I mean is that her breasts were completely exposed, across which an unforgettable pink light was falling out of the lampshade on the bedside table. And her legs were completely open, between which a motley cabbage-like vegetable, shiny like a horse's mane, sprang out abruptly. The only thing that remained on her body was the skirt wrapped around her waist. Higher up, her hair tumbled like dark water on the lilac pillow, and in the middle of all that hair that trembled like foam, like a dance, a red, wide, wet, extensive tongue came out, and that tongue begged to lick, begged for another tongue like hers, wanted to open all her hot pores and bite and squeeze into them another tongue, to knead another animal inside her mouth.

But Juan Carlos was in no hurry to receive that delivery. Supported on one ridiculous knee, his own mass made it difficult for him to pull off his pants. As he moved, the light from the bedside table would sometimes make his damp flaccid face glow like a sponge. Finally his pants gave way, but the movements he made as he wriggled them down to his socks

216

were heavy, millimetric, and now her hands joined her tongue and touched the sweat under his arm and that black curtain was still up there at the headboard, and then Gordo pulled hard on his underpants, and now his pecker popped out, vibrant, granite, as if it had jumped out of one of those spring boxes, just like those clowns that jolt up in those surprise packages. A pecker that was like the entirety of Gordo himself: wide and short. In other words, if you've seen Gordo, you wouldn't have needed any further description to make a drawing of his dick.

But all, absolutely all, of the above (apart from the fact that his pecker was quickly lost inside that precious vegetable) could not compare to the magnificent white surface that was his ass that began to wobble over that electric field that was the brunette down there beneath him.

I have never seen a more powerful, whiter, springier ass in my life. A huge, glorious, accordion-like rump that squeezed and contracted like the heart of a wild beast.

Juan Carlos's ass was an absolutely blissful ass.

Hernán González was now by my side and in the quick sidelong glance I gave him I saw him balancing somewhere between fascination and annoyance.

"Asshole," he said. "I think we're fucking up."

"What?" I asked, as I watched the feats that this backside was capable of when it was infused with motion.

"It's a bunch of bullshit that we're watching Gordo do this," he declared as if in a trance.

I gulped as I saw her belly rise half a meter while her shoulders were still glued to the bed.

"Let's get out of here," I said.

"Let's go."

There's a general strike on November 19, but our parents still send us to school. There are teachers who don't miss a day even if they're dying. That same day Gordo gets another couple of sevens in English class. He was scribbling who knows what on a sheet of notebook paper when Mr. Smith appeared in the aisle and gently tapped him on the shoulder with a pointer. Then he tucked his pointer under his arm like a music hall singer and insinuatingly thrust the right side of his hip forward.

"*May I know what you are writing, Mr. Osorio?*" he said in English.

"*No thing,*" Gordo replied, his English creaky.

Smith hinted at washing that horrid utterance out of his ear, but what he actually did was pinch one of his earlobes. Looking him in the eye, he picked up Juan Carlos's notebook as if pulling on a rat's tail:

"May I see it?"

Gordo shrugged and looked away. Right then he noticed a boy beckoning to him on the other side of the window. Gordo pointed to his chest with a finger and raised his eyebrows, inquiring if he was trying to get his attention. At the window the other said yes with a lurid finger.

"What's this, Good Heaven?" Smith declared pompously, pulling out a regular-sized photo from between the pages of his notebook.

Juan Carlos ignored the photo and in the blink of an eye caught a glimpse of the boy outside holding a battery-operated radio to his ear and pointing to the device with his free hand.

I was Gordo's bench mate now. I felt his desperate knee and stood up, fixing the knot of my tie. He, by *he* I mean *me*, had a seven in English, *he* was above average, not because of Shakespeare, but through Nat King Cole, Brenda Lee, and the Beatles.

"That's a photograph, Mr. Smith."

The teacher froze his face and raised his upper lip a thousandth of a millimeter. If you looked through a magnifying glass it would have been a smile.

He put the photo under the tip of my nose and indicated with his eyebrows that I should look at it.

"I know is a photo. But who are the characters, for God sake?"

Even with the image so close to my eyes I could see that it was a simple filthy box camera photo, one of those that professionals take in the squares with straw hats, white aprons, and about a century and a half of placid provincial life in the galaxy. And Gordo appeared there hugging a blonde and the blonde was also hugging Gordo and passing her hand over his back. I looked at Juan Carlos and handed the photo back to Smith.

"The characters are Juan Carlos Osorio and a girlfriend, sir," I said.

I felt a second knee-blow on my thigh. Before Smith started fanning himself with the photo, I continued:

"Sir, Osario says he's very sorry but he has to leave right now because he feels extremely sick!"

I told Gordo:

"You can leave now."

He got up and wheeled dreamily down the aisle toward the door. Smith followed him with his eyes, and when Gordo had left, Smith brought his nose close to my eyes, dropped the photograph on the bench, and then untucked his pointer and made a band leader–like pirouette.

"*It's curious*," he said.

He then scratched one of his upper teeth with the tip of his fingernail and put the pointer on my shoulder.

"Sit down."

We were out on break eating a sandwich that Dorfman had cut up to share with me when we saw Gordo approaching us with big, chubby strides followed by the kid with the radio.

"Go to the gym!" he said.

We followed him with the battery-powered radio turned off. The Beatles were just getting started and we were hearing the Beatles almost as much as we were breathing. It was strange to see a hand without a transistor radio that first month of school. Eventually the inspectors launched a raid and all those confiscated radios had to be retrieved by our parents.

When we closed the locker room door, the radio guy set up a kind of barricade with the pommel horse and me and González sat on it immediately.

Juan Carlos turned the volume up on the transistor and practically shoved it into our ears.

"Listen," he said.

At first we understood absolutely nothing. The only thing we could make out was that the announcer sounded like he was being strangled. He seemed to be speaking into a microphone and telephone at the same time. There was also a lot of noise in the background, just like when the programs end on TV and those crazy stripes appear on the screen and there's that *chrrrr* sound. I'd only heard so much static on the radio once before, and that was when there was that big earthquake in the south and they reported everything over the phone. That little noise on the radio makes my hair stand on end.

"Listen," Gordo said, his round eyes squeezed tightly between his cheekbones and eyebrows, while he used his fingers to search for a tiny dot on the dial that would fine-tune the transmission.

"What's going on, Gordo?" Dorfman said, pushing the radio away a little. "You can't hear shit."

Juan Carlos grabbed the transistor from between us and turned it off just as he began to speak.

"Comrades," he said. "The government fired on the workers. They killed eight villagers in Caro. They killed them, comrades."

"Why?"

"They put dunnage across the railroad track. Because of the national strike. The government only wants to make a fifteen percent readjustment."

I never thought Gordo could move around a small room so quickly. Interestingly enough, he didn't sweat at all. His face, mind you, was compressed like a bullet and his tongue was sticking out excitedly, moistening his lips, and his Adam's apple was dancing up and down. He slammed his fist across the gap in the stool that González and I had left between us.

"Are we going to put up with this?" he shouted. "There's a national strike to get the government to pay fifty percent. There's a national strike and we're here fucking around!"

My finger was up my nose and Dorfman was spellbound studying Juan Carlos's fisticuffs on the stool. The kid with the radio put it back up to his ear.

"Are we going to let those bastards kill our brothers while we stand here jerking each other off?"

I wiped my sweaty hands on my pants.

"No," I heard myself say.

"No," I repeated, now looking at Gordo and jumping to the floor.

And then I said, "Of course not," looking at Dorfman and González.

Then González:

"Of course not."

And Dorfman:

"No fucking way."

Guatón stepped forward and extended his chubby, vigorous hand to each of us, one by one. I had the impression that I had seen this scene in a movie. I thought the first time I'd said "no" it was because Gordo was outraged and he was my buddy and I wasn't just going to leave him on his own like that. I thought the second time I said "no" it was because I wanted to impress González and Dorfman. But I glimpsed something different when I said "of course not" and jumped to the ground; something leapt out at me from the pit of my stomach, a fist swiping at me, its fingers searing my throat.

Juan Carlos gave us a good looking-over and, before speaking, he bit the tip of his tongue and pushed the empty space in front of him with his hands as if he were testing its density.

"The people are up in arms everywhere. In Dávila, in Feria, in La Esperanza. And in Lo Valledor, too. They've erected barricades with stones and cement blocks.

He paused to take a deep breath.

"Let's...put...an...end...to...this...shit."

Gordo syllabified it without any apparatus. He even continued to reach out for the air with his hands. As if he were holding it so it wouldn't spill out.

"As soon as break is over, go to the second floor and go through the ranks of the sixth years. Dorfman the fifth years, and González and I will take care of the assholes. Tell them: we are going on strike. Tell them: they should gather in the courtyard. Go through the classes quickly and shout out that this is an order from the Student Center. Send them down to the courtyard!"

Strangely enough, all five of us were straightening our hair or rubbing our hands together.

"Send everyone down to the courtyard," I repeated.

González:

"And then what?"

Gordo:

"Then I'm going to speak to them from the second floor."

We all looked at each other for a fraction of a second.

"Gordo, it's not so easy to get into this school. You're new, and if you get into politics, well…"

Dorfman:

"They're going to kick you the fuck out, Gordo."

Guatón smoothed down his hair with both hands and then crossed his short arms over his abundant chest.

"After I speak we'll gather at the corner of Alameda for the parade. Get going!" Gordo said.

As I ran down the stairs I remembered that I hadn't eaten my piece of the sandwich. I used to get insanely hungry around that time. But right then, I wouldn't have been able to eat an olive. I wanted to drink water, a pitcher of water, one of those silver pitchers that get wet on the outside and it's nice to touch them and wipe the moisture off them.

I walked through the ranks of the sixth-year math class, bumping their elbows as I passed.

"Strike now, comrades! Go down to the courtyard! By order of the Student Center!"

As I walked along, some of the bigger, dumb-ass bullies slapped me on the head and the younger ones in line kicked me in the ass and then acted like dicks.

By the time I reached the end of the double row, the most interested kids had crowded behind me.

I shouted dramatically, watching out of the corner of my eye to make sure the superintendent wasn't coming.

"Strike now, comrades! The government has committed murder! By order of the Student Center! Go down to the courtyard immediately!"

A dark-haired guy with a shiny, aquiline nose stood next to me. They called him the Raven, and he was the leader of 5F.

"Everybody down there now," he shouted. "No more classes!"

Without looking at me, he grabbed my elbow and whispered before continuing to yell:

"I'll *mobilize* these assholes."

As I walked down the sixth-year Humanities line, I kept repeating the word "mobilize" to myself. I danced up and down the rows with it. It sounded dramatic, adultlike. It felt rich and elaborate in my mouth like a cool shirt in summer. I knew it was stuck on my tongue and that it would be hard to get it off of there.

"Strike!" I said. "Everyone down to the courtyard immediately! By order of the Student Center!"

I assembled the two rows in a disorganized mass in the middle of the hallway.

"Downstairs!" I shouted. "The government murdered workers at José María Caro. By order of the Student Center! Downstairs! Mobilize!"

I watched the boys spill out in a stampede down the stairs.

I ran my hand over my mouth. Alone in the hallway, as the assholes were taking off like a herd of cattle followed by cowboys, *bang bang bang* and *woop-woop*, I said to myself:

"Ready, Gordo."

A short time later, Gordo's expulsion was decided. The rector told him in person when the barrier we formed around Juan Carlos flanked his entrance. Charge: incitement of violence, promotion of strikes, and insolence toward the authorities.

Juan Carlos scrutinized the rector's patronizing gestures as if he were watching a puppet show on TV.

There were no assholes left inside the school, not even for show. From above, we watched the fireworks display of kids explode, shirtless and disheveled.

Gordo kept looking at the rector, but he didn't really see him. I realized that I was now going over everything he himself had said. That he was thinking about the end of his speech. From a social, and even a theatrical point of view, it was really strange that he walked away while the rector was still speaking to him. He tucked his rolls of fat back into his pants and said, as if he had just remembered:

"Excuse me, sir, but I have to go to the corner."

I remember because of what followed and also because that was one of the last times I saw Juan Carlos in my life.

What followed was that when the old man was left without an audience, we, the ones who were showing our faces, paid the price.

"You, gentlemen," the rector said, "are suspended for one week and you will return with your parents."

At the corner, Gordo sent half of the group to Ahumada and the other half to Moneda. He told them: "Shout loud, you faggots!"

He bought a sandwich layered thick with ham and as we walked in front of the biggest assholes he butchered it with a couple of bites. I waved away his hand when he put what was left over next to my mouth.

"Gordo," I said. "The mobilization was really something."

He shifted the mass of dough he was chewing from one cheek to the other and swallowed long and hard:

"That's nothing. Now comes the good part. The cops are going to come and beat the shit out of us."

He craned his neck to look at me and spoke to me, both amused and serious.

"Do you care if you die?"

I acted like I needed to lean against a wall to keep from fainting.

"*Che*, Gordo," I spoke like an Argentine compadre. "I don't get this philosophy stuff, you know?"

"I'm being serious."

"Well, die of what? Sick or something?"

"No, just from getting beaten up."

I felt like we were walking really fast and a trickle of sweat was dripping down from my armpit. He was as light and bouncy as a kangaroo. A gorgeous woman passed me and looked at me for an eternally long second and I felt awesome.

"Look, Gordo. The truth is that I'd prefer not to die. I'd also prefer not to have the shit kicked out of me. I'd rather spend my life banging beautiful chicks like her."

Juan Carlos used his shirtsleeve to wipe away his sweat and didn't even look at me when he spoke again.

"And do you know what I think?"

"About dying or not dying?"

"Yes."

I happily wiped my hands on my pants.

"You don't give a shit," I answered.

Gordo smiled.

"That is, you're a *guataca*, a sycophant," I added. "You don't give a shit about any of this. You don't give a damn."

"Exactly."

"Because I've realized something about you, Gordo. You're a Marxist agitator."

"Exactly."

"Do you know why?"

"Because the exploiters are a bunch of sons of bitches."

Without breaking his stride, he held out his spacious, sweaty hand to me.

"Comrade," he said.

By one o'clock that afternoon we had been meticulously pummeled and were studying our wounds in the calaboose. My best contribution was the non-visible traces of a dry and penetrating nightstick blow between my shoulder and neck. It landed there, I remember, when I made a slight maneuver to save my ear. When I lifted my shirt collar and pulled it to the right, the spectacle of a violet stain emerged; it was as thick as a plate and sad like a ring. Juan Carlos studied it with the indifference of a nurse, or a bartender, and said:

"Sons of bitches."

More to encourage me than to bitch and moan. As payment in kind I had to comment on the bruise above his eyelid. Incidentally, his had a better angle, since the nightstick blow had somehow splintered part of his nose. And although the blood had dried, there was still a lumpy red scab. I didn't know which was more serious, a purple splotch like this or a bump on the forehead plus a scab on the nose.

When my old man came to get me out, I took it for granted that Osorio would also be released. We even walked together from the cell to the lobby. Then my old man signed I don't know what the fuck, whacked me across the face, which I received with a grunt, and then turned around to look at Osorio.

"Not that one," he said to the lieutenant. He added:

"That's Juan Carlos Osorio."

His voice seemed magical, swollen. It hit me that the lieutenant was a priest and had just given Mass. It hit me that Gordo was chubby like all the little Jesus babies I had seen. I approached him all ceremoniously and held out my hand.

"They screwed you, Gordo."

El Guatón adjusted his rolls of fat as best he could and pressed his lips together tightly, and his cheekbones looked comical and spongy like Danny Kaye's when he plays the clown. When he shook my hand he moved his jaw proudly.

"I'm hungry," he said.

He gave my old man's hand a meaningful look as he squeezed my elbow to walk me away.

"We got our asses handed to us, Gordo."

"Like I told you."

"Like you told me."

I held out my hand again and we had a long, senti-mental handshake.

Two weeks later I was enrolled in the party and had formed a group at the Lyceum. González, Dorfman, Llanos, Petit Fleur Millar, and Escobedo were there. Before the summer break we had created a political library made up of thirty books, and we held meetings at my house every Saturday. In March we voted for the Student Center and we chose Millar with seventy percent of the votes. Petit Fleur remains in charge of the School Central and all of us in sixth year go out to work in the villages. The teachers treat me with respect and I walk around with *Granma*, the Cuban newspaper, and *Marcuse* under my arm.

The presidential elections are two years later and we suffer a setback. Frei wins. This is '64. I'm a brilliant university student and I'm in a relationship with a girl. In '66 the government slaughters work-ers in El Salvador. In '69 they massacre settlers in a working-class neighborhood in Puerto Montt. That same year I am elected party youth leader of the entire country.

We win the presidential elections with Chicho Allende in 1970 and I already have a son. I, who have been a leader in the university and the party, end up as Intendant in the south of Chile. I'm the youngest asshole in such a responsible position. We've been governing for months and the opposition hasn't found any way to deal us a coup d'état. Nothing! We nationalize their copper, we liquidate their monopolies, we convert their banks to government ownership, we transfer factories to the social sector, we control their dollars, we redistribute their income. The right-wingers are desperate.

In the south, I have problems with a line of MIR, the Revolutionary Left Movement comrades who want to run the process their way. We have laws in accordance with our analysis. I have a big problem: the minister isn't taking care of this mess because of all the work he has. Yesterday the Nazis killed a Mapuche and all hell broke loose in a whorehouse with the MIR bastards in violent protest. Conclusion: uniformed members of the *carabitate* police force tell me that they're bringing in someone from the MIR who wants to discuss some proposals with me.

I go into my office, light a cigarette, and then ask them to bring him in.

A lieutenant comes in, and just behind him Juan Carlos Osorio.

A lieutenant comes in, and just behind him Juan in his dark gray trousers. He wears flip-flops and has dirty feet, just like the peasants in this region. Just like the peasants, he wears a white shirt without a tie and the collar folded inward.

I know this is totally sentimental, but my knees buckle a little. My stomach and balls are tight. I flick the ash outside the ashtray and say to the policeman:

"Thank you, Lieutenant."

He leaves a file on the table, puts his hand to his cap, and walks out saluting.

I rush over to Gordo and we embrace properly. And we part to show each other our wide, proud necks, and when I put my hands on Juan Carlos's flabby shoulders he seems to feel wider to me.

I speak:

"Whores, comrade."

Juan Carlos:

"Whores, compadre."

I speak:

"Don't fuck it up, comrade."

He speaks:

"Sir, don't fuck it up yourself, compadre."

He sits at one end of the desk without asking. I walk over to the armchair and also sit down.

And there we sit, looking at each other.

man with a carnation
in his mouth

I feel yearnings, desires
But not with my whole being. Something
Deep inside me, something there,
Cold, heavy, mute remains.

FERNANDO PESSOA

The girl skirted the trees with the speedy momentum of a woman alone in a public place, between dignified, cautious, and distracted, as if solitude were something to be ashamed of and the mouths of every man were about to come lick her neck or bite her lips.

She feigned that look of having a specific destination in mind until she had crossed the width of the plaza. When she reached the edge, she stopped and took a deep breath. Her shoulders relaxed, her chin fell into a smile, and her elbows eased into an encouraging gesture to herself. She had once again been surprised by the tensions and formalities she despised, by the distrust, by the misery of artifice in her face, by the selfishness of useless dignities. She thought: "I walked home from school like this. I walked to the movies on Sunday like this. All women walk like this. As if being alone somehow turned us into whores."

The men and women in the plaza raised their wrists and focused their attention on the hour. They compared watches, glanced at the side streets, looked up at the sky as if hoping all that restlessness were moored to something. They were together, but in the way that those who survive a lively party stay together slapping the tonearm of the record player when there's not enough music to make everyone happy. Only seconds remained and no one wanted to send off the old year as nonchalantly as dropping a letter in the mailbox.

They looked around the corners again. They were also adamant about the sky, raised their wrists to their ears, and the girl felt the breeze rustle the flower over her ear.

That's when she knew there was a man behind her.

And in the exact second of all the hugs, she also knew that this was the man who was hugging her; not with a frontal, strident, and emphatic New Year's hug, but with a half hug, an insinuation, like someone hangs on a familiar shoulder, but also with the gentleness of someone who knows that shoulder is fragile.

She wanted to remain in that ignorant and amused silence, caught up in that anonymous acquisition, give up on the rest of the scene, the characters, the decorations of surreal lights, the city, Portugal and the galaxy, but she had already twisted her neck and was glancing around, a slight tension in her eyes, at the features of the boy who gave her only a distracted smile, relaxed, accidental, as if he had been hanging on her shoulder for three nights in a row and, already tired of chatting with her, was pondering the small eccentricities of the passersby, the shouts and the greetings, as if he were a judge of shouts and greetings.

With great dexterity, the young man pinned the stem of the carnation in his mouth with his tongue, and with a curious pirouette deposited it between his lips in the left corner of his mouth. He held it there with his jaw clenched.

That was the moment when the girl amended "Happy New Year" in her mind and let her own fluency speak for her.

"In case you didn't know, that's my shoulder," she said.

"Yeah, I know," the young man (younger than her) mumbled, without looking at her (but managing to look at her). "I'm hanging on yours because I'm not interested in mine anymore."

He held the stem of the carnation between his teeth so he could talk to her. She raised her free hand and poked at the flower with a finger.

"I'm guessing you're a vegetarian, right?"

"No, I don't eat them. I just put them in my mouth."

The frenzied crowd in the plaza began to flood toward the left corner. From a side street, preceded by honking horns that accompanied the refrain "The people...united...will never be defeated," a chaotic line of students and workers advanced. They both let themselves be carried forward by the wave and they walked along the curb until they joined the front of the march. An old man with a pointed nose, bulky glasses, and a visible limp in his stride held the pole of a huge red flag. Although the people applauded him with fervor as he passed, the man seemed absent, haloed with some small glory, attentive to some symphonic music that issued only in his own head.

They marched a little in front of him, without letting go of each other, while in the plaza rounds of the same refrain were being composed. There were dripping bottles everywhere. They came out of car windows or were leaked in by flag-waving cyclists. The sound of champagne popping open was isolated among the shouts, chants, and horns, all stirred by a breeze that was hardly cool at all, exactly as if it were not winter.

The young man pulled her aside and into the Piquenique restaurant and told her to sit at the lunch counter. They ordered two sandwiches and a select bottle of red wine.

"Well," he said, "my name's Jorge."

"Carmen," the young woman said.

Their hands touched, clasped, and they waited for the wine in silence. In the interval they looked each other over a little with amused smiles and vague gestures. She concluded that it wasn't the young man's style to ask any more questions, though it was hers. But in the end, she didn't ask him anything either. The wine arrived and they drank the first glass with

243

knowing speed. The girl savored the taste and the warmth on her cheekbones. He collapsed in laughter on the counter and buried his face in his arms. He shook for a few seconds as she poured two new measures, then he lifted his face and wiped his wet cheeks. He placed the carnation in the gap between his front teeth, imperfect, and nodded to himself, trying hard not to laugh anymore.

"I'm really happy...*muy contento*," he said in Spanish.

"I can see that," the young woman said.

"I was in prison for a year. My old man was imprisoned for five years, until he escaped from jail. He died in France."

The girl invited him with her eyebrows to raise his wineglass. The steaming sandwiches were placed on the counter, and they ate them with avidity. When only a few scattered crumbs remained and the waiter had emptied the bottle, filling their glasses with professional dexterity, the boy said:

"I'll pay now, and we'll go home. You'll stay over and sleep with me."

He awaited the reaction to the news with excessive vigilance, not his style at all. He stretched his lips to show all his teeth crowned by the red carnation in the middle gap.

"I don't want to," the girl said.

"Don't you like me?"

"No, I do like you."

"What then?"

"I don't want to."

The young man pulled on his hair.

"What's happened is that you got mad at me because I didn't take the carnation out of my mouth."

She regretted that there was nothing left in her glass. The young man handed her his and the girl sipped a little, suddenly serious. He tapped a crumb with one finger and pushed it into the palm of his other hand.

"I made a promise when the fascists were toppled that I'd spend the first night of the year with a carnation in my mouth," he said, gently picking at his ear. "I can sleep with you, but I couldn't kiss you or lick you because of this little problem."

The girl scratched her head. She knew that in the smile with which she was now looking at him, she had just disappointed him.

"I can't," she said.

Unzipping a pouch full of small bills, the young man paid the check.

They walked, among shreds of noisy parades and persistent slogans, apart, in a silence that he accentuated with his lowered head and his hands thrust deep into his pockets. Just outside her hotel, the girl decided to console him:

"I have a five-year-old son. He's with me in the room."

He kicked an imaginary ball and shrugged.

"Your husband, too?"

"No. I'm a widow."

"What then?"

They were at the door. She said:

"Good night." He said:

"Good night."

And he turned his back on her unequivocally.

The last sight of him the girl had was his tangled hair merging at the corner with the weary tranvía 11, Graça. She deftly pulled out a cigarette and then raised a distinct flame to it.

The maid was on her bed reading a love story.

"Everything's fine, ma'am," she said, anticipating. "Everything's perfect."

"He didn't wake up?"

"Not even a little."

"I don't know how to thank you."

"Please, ma'am! Was the plaza pretty?"

"Yes," she said.

"Did you go for a walk?"

"Yes."

"New year, new life, isn't that right?"

"It was very pretty."

The maid yawned suddenly and tried to disguise it with a little chirp. The girl unbuttoned her blouse and put the cigarette on the edge of the ashtray.

"What time are you leaving?"

"At ten. Wake me at eight, please."

"Of course. And where are you going, ma'am?"

"To Romania."

The girl shook the woman's hand at the door.

"You were very kind. I appreciate it."

"See you tomorrow, ma'am."

The maid went down the steps and started to turn out the lights in the reception area. She had only just passed the lobby doorknob when she noticed a young man with a carnation in his mouth peeping through the outer part of the entranceway. Without knocking,

he indicated with a curled finger that she should un-
bolt the door. The woman turned her ear toward him,
curious and reticent.

"A young lady," the young man said through the
glass.

"I don't remember her name. She has a son."

"Yes," the maid said, "the Chilean."

The young man looked at her gravely and blinked
abundantly. With a haphazard hand movement, he
tried to gather the hair that was spilling over his forehead, but to no avail.

"Exactly," he said. "The Chilean. I have to go up
and see her."

"She's already in bed."

"That's okay, it doesn't matter. Let me in."

The maid unbolted the door and the boy scram-
bled up the first few steps.

"Look, she must be asleep by now."

"What room?" the young man shouted from the
second floor.

"Eleven," the maid said, leaning into the stairway.

The young man knocked on the door but didn't
wait for an answer. He turned the doorknob and
barged into the room. The girl turned around naked,
except for the small panties she was about to slip over

her hips. The young man advanced without hesitation and took the flower out of his mouth. He put it in the vase, along with the other carnations. He looked at the young woman's small breasts and plunged his hands back into his pockets.

"Okay," he said, before leaving the room, "next time be more explicit."

Setúbal, Portugal, 1975

from blood
to oil

A drizzly morning in Rome. For the passenger in the taxi, memories of movies from the last decade. Something like Antonioni on the roads. Considering things after the fact, the flat tire could have been a harbinger of something to come. The driver, reckless, changed the tire not too far off the asphalt. The same disorder as in all of Rome, its exuberance, its out-of-order telephones, its multitudes of priests and soldiers on every street.

At 12:15, the airport. A monotonous circus of metal and glass full of kiosks with dazzling and useless trinkets appreciated indifferently by businessmen, pale teenagers, angry Americans scattering the youth in a Europe that repeats itself day in and day out. And white Arab robes in solemn abundance.

LH 303. The green boarding pass. A thousand-lira airport fee and the employee's voice: "Gate ten or eleven. The flight is a little late." 10 or 11, LH 303, 12:35 p.m.! Figures that don't tolerate frenzy, clues contemporary society clings to in a photograph. The sweet precision of a world of executives and executors. A planet that is a compact body but filled with oil instead of blood. The liquid flows smoothly from the storage tanks to the airplanes parked on the tarmac. I remembered the old Frankie Laine song in *Blowing Wild* (That's right, my friend, Gary Cooper and Barbara Stanwyck!): *And this girl loved me back, loved me more, more than black gold*. It was easy, and uncertain, to wander through the airport's electronic doors now that no one could love anyone else but black gold.

I saw the Lufthansa flight arrive and settle on the tarmac while a last call for the Pan Am flight boiled over the loudspeakers. I watched the passengers of LH 303 disembark with that envious look that the departing passengers give to the arriving ones. I thought they would take longer to call us. I toyed with the idea of going to the restaurant to try a ravioli dish, but I changed my mind. Rome has never brought me any luck and the wishful coins I tossed into the Trevi Fountain have never been generous to the whims of

my destiny. (It was a day for the movies. The Four
Aces? Romanticolor and Clifton Webb?) I decided I
should go through the security check for carry-on luggage and pass through the arch of the metal detector
right away. An achievement with a particular amount
of suspense we all get through with a droplet of pride.
When I came out the policeman patted the coins in
the right pocket of my pants. They jingled a little song.

Money, the guard said. I smiled at him. I'm always
really kind to people who do jobs I would never in
my life want to do. And that smile undermined him
because he stood there sighing as I walked away.
"Money, money, money."

Immediately after, exploratory glances at the
passengers. Several familiar faces, the same ones I'd
encountered at the Sorrento Film Festival a few days
before. Standing tall, slender, and dressed like a model
for advertisements, a woman leaned against the windows overlooking the tarmac. I thought that I'd like to
meet her, that she'd be some actress recovering from
her festival hangover at the airport. Another woman
I did know was an actress passed through the security
checkpoint. She was weighed down by a kilo of sophis-
tication and as soon as I saw her I remembered that
she'd exchanged addresses with a French dandy in

Naples. I hadn't forgotten her because while she was talking to him she kept taking off her glasses and putting them back on in a rather dreadful fashion. I find nothing to appreciate about the others: people like me who belong to the opaque community of irrelevant passengers.

Out of the blue I remembered that I'd forgotten my favorite shirt on the bathroom counter in my motel room. I thought that I really wouldn't want to lose it, so I decided to phone a friend at the motel so he could send it to Munich. I set off for the metal detector. The next day I read in the newspapers that it was 12:51. The 12:35 LH 303 was sixteen minutes late at gate 10. I think I took a step forward. Or I backed up. A large group of people were around the entrance to the archway.

And then the shot. One. And then another, another, and one more. And glass shattering. The strained sound of something splintering. I'd never seen fire come out of a gun from in front of it before. In the movies, anyway. Had it even lasted a second?

Still standing by the windows on the left side of the room, I thought for a moment that the activity had something to do with the kidnapping of Paul Getty, the one the mafia had released in Naples just two days earlier. I assumed it would be the gangsters running off with the ransom money, or a bank robbery. In any case I had the absurd confidence that everything would end later on. In none of the films do the police let their quarry escape at the airport. But, as if to disprove that theory, the shooting raged on. I saw that almost all the passengers had thrown themselves to the floor. I got the impression that the shooting was indiscriminate, that there wasn't a single target. That in truth, the bullets were being raffled off. And then I stretched out on the floor, my head sheltered behind a metal shelf.

I looked behind me and I saw what panic really looks like. I understood why filmmakers never get these scenes right. Panic makes no noise. Panic is a frantic silence that spills from eyes, from tense mouths and uncertain, trembling noses. In the midst of panic we are all children of the same final silence. Dismayed children of mother machine gun and father silence, with a gesture that means: "Hand this to me, airplane passenger, proper citizen, punctual in your payment of debts, film festival, honest salesman." With their necks stretched to the limit, everyone expected someone from the airline company, prompt, uniformed, efficient, to come and solve this little blip in the itinerary. "This way, please, *por favor, prego, bitte, s'il vous plaît*."

And problems of panic are not metaphysical; stomach to the floor, cheek on the tile, I assessed whether the piece of furniture protecting me would give any resistance to the bullets. I deduced no. That the bullets would go through light metal like bodies and wood. That we were on the floor because that way we were harder targets to hit, but by no means were we safe. I didn't rule out that they also shot at the floor. At the time we hadn't yet bought the next day's newspapers with the Fiumicino massacre on the front page. The bullets and revolvers had no name at that point. A projectile without a last name, but with a capricious destination that could be my head.

Now the shooting was building up and happening all over again in the fragile departure lounge box. I sensed that we were all feeling the same way. That there would be a shoot-out between the police and "the others," in this same lounge, and that it would be over when all our bodies were shot to bits. I raised my head slightly and looked over my shoulder.

And that's when I saw that guy. Standing up, almost with his hands in his pockets, almost smoking a cigarette butt on his favorite neighborhood street corner, absorbed and amazed by the shooting, almost as if it happened in some distant country, with slightly amused eyebrows, as if saying to himself they're screwing with us, this is a hoax, it's *Candid Camera*, it's all part of some feverish young director's imagination.

My scream and the ammunition flying around him roused him from his daydream. Then he dropped to the floor and crawled behind a column. Now, abruptly, the front window was SHATTERED BY SHOTS! Immediately after, a burly man wearing a light raincoat finished breaking the glass with his body and jumped through gate 10 onto the jet bridge that led to the slab of concrete, the apron, where the planes were parked.

I was afraid when I saw that. I thought I was engaging with something extremely dangerous and isolated. I curled up more tightly on the floor. I didn't want to look around anymore. Then came silence. A pause that seemed definitive. Behind me there was a group of five people behind a column and among them a little six-year-old boy. We stood up in silence and walked around a little, almost crouching. And there the other noises exploded. Not bullets now. They seemed like bombs. Someone howled something in German about airplanes. A new shower of bullets rained down on the lounge, this time coming from the apron. I grabbed the little one and covered him with my body. I thought it was useless, that the projectiles would go through two, three, a thousand bodies.

In the middle of the violent uproar an airline employee pointed to a glass door behind him and urged us to run through it. It led to a promenade, like the one that led to the airplanes, but on the opposite side. A lot of people rushed to the door. The boy was with his father now. Soon everyone was running down the ramp to the outside of the airport.

I stayed where I was, crouched down, thinking that it might not be appropriate to run. That maybe they'd shoot those who ran. The police or whoever the others were. I ridiculously opted for a solution that Peter Sellers would have envied. Something between a fast stride and the beginning of a trot. I think what I had in mind in those last seconds was the "law of the escape." That is, the one that applies to a prisoner when the guards give him a chance to escape only to shoot him in the back, to kill him from behind. That stretch of the apron was now filled with people fleeing from their planes. It was there that I first heard that a plane had burned. From my horizontal position in the glass lounge, I didn't catch any of the action beside the planes. But now I was witnessing the residue of the bombing. Women with their clothes ripped to shreds, the wounded crawling around screaming with their faces and bodies torn apart.

We entered one of the airport blocks. There were several small, sparsely furnished rooms. Posters on the walls. On the longest sofa, two women were crying uncontrollably. One of them was clutching her stomach tightly, as if she were pregnant. I was approached by a Japanese man who wouldn't put his briefcase down, and he spoke to me in English: "Do you think it will take long for things to get back to normal? Do you know what time the train for Milano leaves? Do you know how long the train to Milano takes?"

I shrugged. The father entered with his son. They were French. The man sat the little boy down and wiped off his knees. "You were lucky your daddy was with you, eh?" he said. The boy smiled. The father ran his hand over the boy's head.

Now two large Germans who were on their way to or returning from skiing in Austria came in. One of them, the one weighing around two hundred and fifty pounds, had oil stains on his white raincoat. The other was portly with a stubbly, few-days-old beard. A haughty, curly-haired Greek started a violent shouting match with the big German that I couldn't quite figure out. All I know is that the big man at one point looked at all of us to support what he shouted in English:

"Murderous radicals!" I was struck by how the term "radicals" applied to our context. The fat man with the unkempt beard described two of "them," and made a gesture of someone shooting a machine gun. One of the women stopped crying and looked at me with a nervous smile.

Two policemen peeked through the open door and then continued, running. It seemed to me that they were the first agents that I'd seen. I even doubted whether the police had been involved in the shooting. The German with the beard took a whiskey bottle out of his pocket and drank from it prodigiously. We all took a sip, except for the Japanese. I wanted to ask them, one by one, what they had seen. I soon came to the conclusion that panic is blind. No one had seen anything. On top of the facts, they didn't remember one detail. They had only been paying attention to their own terror, their helplessness.

After half an hour we left the room. "All together," shouted the fat German, organizing us. We walked along the back of the apron, and soon we saw the airport's main entrance. Hundreds crowded over the glass doors, watched by security guards, and on top of the access walkways. On the way, there was an unprotected stretch that left a dangerous clearing open to the site where the action took place. A policeman signaled us to move away from there, that we should follow the path in front of us. It would be around 1:30. Now dozens of police cars were coming. Fire trucks. Then soldiers. And ambulances. Lots of ambulances. The old Arabs sat on the curbs and paving stones, speechless. I approached the actress, who was talking to the lanky girl. I said something stupid to identify myself to show I was part of her world: "This film was definitely not presented at Sorrento." She looked at me with distant surprise. (My stock improved only two hours later, when I said I'd seen one of her movies on TV and liked it.) I started hearing what people were talking about. I formed an idea of what had happened from the versions of several unreliable witnesses. There were estimations from ten to a hundred dead. At that very moment the Lufthansa plane was in the black sky, and we watched it long and hard, until it was lost. Then we looked down, searched each other's faces, and assessed our bewilderment.

No one moved. No one proposed anything. Everyone murmured: "The company should do something." After the tempest a viscid refuge. Two hours after the massacre they hardly cared about death, not how many, not which ones, not the cause, not the outcome, not anything. Now everyone was thinking that they were tired, that they were hungry, that they wanted to pee. (Where, where?) They thought the companies weren't doing anything. Not the German, not the Japanese, not the French.

Soon, very soon, they were no longer survivors of some calamity but simply outraged passengers. Preoccupied with their guts, their makeup, and their suitcases. And at that moment something peculiar happened, characteristic perhaps of the ineffable whims of Rome. The security guards opened the doors to one of the entrances to the interior. That was a bit much. Arabs in white headdresses, slender blacks, frail old women, and American brats, tangled in a single wave, swirled toward the "Passport Control" sign, and in a minute they formed lines of avid, ferocious, thirsty airplane consumers, hungry for seat belts, "No Smoking" signs, whiskey and cigarettes at duty-free prices.

That's when I felt like crying. The Rome airport was a metaphor for the universe, for all its races, its clothes, its cultures, its dreams, and now, precisely now that many of them had died, that a few of them had killed, that humanity, that multitudinous

262

existence had no time, no desire, no aptitude, to pass from terror to awe. Everyone returns so quickly to their own navels, their briefcases, their pilgrimages to pray to incomprehensible gods!

That quickly from blood to oil!

I felt angry at myself. For belonging to a species that still gives me hope, despite the massacres that infect the Middle East, and Asia, and Europe, and my wounded America. I felt a long, damp sadness for all our little obligations, sentimental commitments, ideals accommodated to our social and economic security.

And there was still something missing. From the other entrance to the interior, a squad of policemen appeared running with their guns in their hands, shouting and gesturing at the people to get out of there as quickly as possible... who had allowed them to enter. Now running to the exit, passports in hand, panted breathing, stumbling, biting at each other. Once again out to a cloudy day, the abusive smoking, the dry mouth, the hunger, the sticky self-pity of the survivors.

But the actress already had the first newspaper of the afternoon in her hands, and we stretched our necks around the edges of her delicate ears to read what covered the whole front page: MASSACRE IN

FIUMICINO. Then a small, discreet, but unbearable sense of pride arose. Now everyone had something to add to or contradict about the newspaper reports. Within the hour, they had crafted their adventures. Everyone with an air of tired old heroes, of fighters of a battle that they neither lost nor won, nor even fought in or saw.

At six o'clock it was dark. The woman treated me to a sweet that I chewed on greedily and despairingly. The airline counters opened. No one asked the young women from the companies what they knew about their fellow passengers, the flight attendants, the pilot, about the machine itself. They wanted to ignore the issue like some disagreeable mishap, a little adventure that the hours, the days, the years, will enlarge and mythologize, until the time will come when they will be the real heroes for their grandchildren. Maybe at that moment in front of the counter we forget we're asking, "when is the next flight, where is my luggage, will they pay for the hotel, will they send us to the hotel by taxi, will they pay for the food at the hotel."

Yes. They sent us to the hotel in a taxi. And they paid for the food. And a bed at the hotel. "Hotel Satellite." The advertisement says it's five minutes from the airport and ten minutes from the city. It's actually fifteen minutes from the airport and thirty minutes from the city. In limbo. A huge voracious airplane that will never fall from the sky. In the restaurant the table had to be expanded and the receptionists were deliriously handing out keys, writing down passport information. The phones were ringing off the hook. The Satellite, today, was the main planet. At the restaurant table, the lanky girl motioned for me to sit next to her. She told me she was a psychologist.

Just as stupid as before, I told her she looked like an actress. She, desperately wanted to call Munich. I, that the youth of Berlin is so-so. In front of us, along the entire length of the table, were thirty Arabs. There were bottles of red and white wine every two plates. They waited for dinner in silence, drinking mineral water. None of them even touched the wine. Within a couple of minutes, a huge black man harangued them from the head of the table. "I feel like I'm dreaming," a Polish actor to my left said.

When the chicken was served, the Arabs turned their plates upside down in a sign of protest. A stocky one, who saw us hurrying through our bottle of white wine, handed his bottle to me.

"Do you speak Spanish?" he asked. I nodded.

"That's good," he said. "I speak the Spanish."

"Where are you from?" I asked.

"From Maroc."

"Good," I said. "I've been to Ouarzazate, two hundred kilometers south of Marrakech."

I thought: two ministers on the plane.

"I'm from Agadir," a thin Arab said.

"Where did you learn Spanish?"

"In the Spanish Civil War."

"Okay," I said. "Whose side did you fight on?"

The Arab hesitated for a moment and broke off a piece of bread.

"That's a secret between Allah and me."

"Okay," I said, annoyed.

I went to the lounge to watch TV. The adventure belonged to everyone now. The tragedy belonged to everyone. The participants in the drama felt a little robbed of what they'd accomplished, a little tamed by the receiver's images of the real horror. The Polish actor drank a lot in the bar, the psychologist wanted to phone Germany, the Arabs deployed slowly and disappeared, the actress was swallowed up by the night in Rome. I bought a bottle of shampoo so I could wash my hair.

The next day there was another LH flight 303. All of us bought all the Italian newspapers and sat with the thick bundles of paper on our knees. We were back in the waiting room. A pushback tug was slowly pulling the Pan Am jet to the runway. Slow, funereal, an ambulance and two fire trucks followed it.

At the Munich airport, a man approached the actress with a bouquet of flowers, and she pretended not to notice the photographer. The German press delivered the final patina of notoriety, the final detritus of true panic.

Then home. To tell the story. To tell it and retell it. Until it is forgotten.

teresa clavel's
lover

My relationship with Estévez began with something as tenuous as the initial letter of our last names. I'll omit mine because it belongs to the annals of ignominy. Suffice it to say that just as in those school days when the teacher questioned students in pairs by the blackboard, putting them together only because of their consecutiveness in an alphabetical list, likewise Estévez and I were snatched from jail and packed onto a Swissair flight to Zurich, where a group of idealists had appeared before the dictator of our homeland urging him to release us. One tropical rainy day, when the prison director called our names, he did so with a shout that might well have served as the title for this confession: "Estévez and the other one are out."

I'm the other one.

A variable in this turbulent exercise, a wild card in a night of gamblers.

When we landed in the ensuing European drizzle, five or six people were waiting for us on the airport tarmac. A girl wearing something like what a Gypsy would wear, tousled red curls, an emphatic nose, and trinkets on her wrists, held up a sign: "Estévez."

"You must be the other one," she said excitedly, smearing a kiss on each side of the beard that had grown out during my months of captivity.

When they asked about our luggage, Estévez showed them a piece of paper containing only our names and our date of expulsion, and added, with a smile that had a contagious effect:

"This would be all."

"Wretches," the red-haired woman with Lennon glasses roared. "They didn't even let them bring their toothbrushes."

This girl had tremendous energy and a complete lack of humor. When I pulled the comb with exactly five teeth, like those made popular by Billy Bayley, out of the back pocket of my pants, and said: "There's no need to be dramatic. I was allowed to bring this," she looked at me, bitter and troubled.

From the airport we went to a large department store where we tried on pants, shirts, shoes, gym shoes, and a white double-breasted jacket, one that was, ironically, identical in style to the one the officer who arrested me in Port-au-Prince had worn, and then he took me to a secret place, where after a few blows I admitted that I had allowed a man to stay in my apartment, a man they were hard-pressed to bring in. A couple more blows and I suggested that they might find him in a new hiding place. Chance, or his familiarity with my failings, prompted my friend to change his residence and, while they were waiting for me to come up with a more accurate accusation, they kept me in jail for a few months.

That's where I met Estévez.

As a matter of fact, I'd seen him in newspaper photos, his determined chin, that agitated vein along his temple, the eyes of his associates magnetized, but in the reality of the cell he was diminished by the torture, his sadness, the meager food we received, and defeat. The same day I was brought in I noticed his authority. The prisoners wanted to know about my background, presuming that I was a big shot in the failed democracy or an activist in the Lavalas movement. Estévez welcomed me with a hug and handed me a cigarette, which we smoked in slow, fraternal silence. After throwing the cigarette butt through the bars, he wanted to know my name and my affiliation. When I told him I lacked any, he seemed to enjoy my discretion. It was the standard position for all the supporters of the deposed government.

Why'd they put me with him? Me, who would have given anything to appear in the newspapers one day? Soon enough I became infected with the speculations so common to that environment, and one day, in those promiscuities between guards and captives, where the former are ostentatiously "human," I asked Sergeant Couffon about it:

"When the dog's big, what's it matter how big the flea is," he said, gruffly.

In the evenings we listened to a small portable radio that could sometimes pick up signals from abroad. They affirmed the imminence of a popular uprising in Gonaïves, and spoke about campaigns in Europe to demand, among other things, the reinstatement of Aristide and the release of Estévez. That he'd soon be released was clear to me when I noticed that they stopped torturing him and brought him a brush, a razor, and soap. When he was stripped of that tangle of hair and scabs covered his fresh scars, he was a distinguished man of lofty beauty.

Next to him, I looked like an exclamation point after an adjective. I'd been skinny my whole life, and the months I spent in prison had honed this talent to pathetic perfection. In the few rounds of prisoner soccer we played on a field improvised with stones instead of goalposts, Estévez gave words of encouragement to the dejected, handed out a cigarette or two trafficked in who knows what operation, recited some futuristic paragraph that minimized the catastrophe they were suffering, listened with an intensity bordering on fervor to the litanies of his fellow inmates. It was as if he had naturally assumed the position of a prison imam. As if some unspoken election had appointed him president of these shadows.

As for me, I spent my hours amused by my lack of any kind of background. Neither in the days prior to the overthrow, nor in my captivity, had the deposed Jean-Bertrand Aristide relied upon my support or interest. His utopian sympathizers caused me as much abysmal grief as his brutal detractors. That among so many vociferous people I had fallen into prison with my pusillanimous silence could be interpreted as an irony that

even my guards ended up understanding. I could en-
liven their interrogations only with a little imagination,
for I held nothing nourishing in my saddlebag. No one
asked my name in prison, not so much out of discretion
as out of disinterest. When they called me, they did so
with a generic nickname, one with which I felt—at least
I thought so at the time—comfortable: "Skinny." They
didn't know how humiliated I felt when they asked me
if any of my achievements in the resistance had been
written about in any newspaper.

One Saturday morning a French politician's visit
was announced for noon that day and we were each
given a piece of soap and a minute under the shower.
That brief occasion acquainted me with the sores on
Estévez's body, but also with his sexual attributes. I
failed to specify at that moment the meaning of the
pleasant emotion that permeated my being: in precisely this category I could compete with Estévez as
an equal, and depending on the inflections in the
moment, perhaps I'd even have an advantage. This re-
alization invigorated me as much as the bone-chilling
jets of frigid water. I just hadn't yet figured out how to
follow up on this relative talent.

The contemptible occasion began to germinate
in Switzerland. Our incandescent hosts were by no

means in charge. Their meager influence was ob-
tained by squeezing religious coffers, humanitarian
conglomerates, official politicians to whom a dissi-
dent tinge was convenient, and the hearts of well-
intentioned boys, who, convinced that carrying out a
revolution in their country was as dangerous as it was
impossible, projected their utopias on distant revolts,
whose detritus they then collected with unction. It's
only natural that the State should rein in these fiery
colts. To be allowed free movement around the Swiss
cantons, we had to spend a period of time in a refugee
camp in a small town, where our past and present
intentions were checked and we were helped to define
an honorable future. Medical exams, political background checks, elementary language classes, psycho-
therapy, that was our routine for the three months
before we were allowed to go out and contaminate
their cities.

Precarious destiny continued to bind us together.
The rooms were designed for two applicants, and neither Estévez nor I had any reason to dispense with the
other. On the contrary, our language ignorance could
be doubled if we were put in the room of a Polish,
Nigerian, or Vietnamese person. The reception com-
mittee came to make their inquiries into our territory.

They started with Estévez. I was leafing through a
Paris Match the local priest brought me; he was accompanying a translator who was already infected by
a few patois twists heard at the airports. The official
looked at me sympathetically and asked Estévez if
he preferred to speak with him in privacy. He simply
raised his shoulders: it was all the same to him. After
ten minutes of somewhat puerile medical ramblings (if
he'd had chicken pox, whooping cough, measles, if his
foreskin was hooded or cut), he got to the point. What
had Estévez done to merit being granted political
asylum?

A blessed rosary wouldn't have as many beads as
my comrade in captivity had accounts: leader of an
insurrectionary party during high school, teacher of
theory to military officers, organizer of neighborhood
councils, executor of a worker-peasant alliance capable of paralyzing the country in a couple of hours, and
(I stopped looking at the *Paris Match* photos) lover of
Teresa Clavel, celebrated princess of the underground,
so nicknamed because of the last photo of her published by the press, with a red flower in her mouth,
before she plunged into her perilous lawlessness.

Then it was my "turn." My account was not only
meager, but imprudent. In my case, it wasn't a matter

of demonstrating "good" conduct to the official, but quite the opposite. A guarantee for the granting of asylum was that our lives were in danger in our home country. At a moment when I was transitioning from one boring monosyllable to another, Estévez intervened, saying that my "modesty" was already pathological, and transformed my brief accommodation of someone who didn't want to spend a tense night at home into a brave gigantomachia. Even so, the official and his translator didn't seem convinced that I should be granted asylum. "You are very nice," the translator said. And he added in a colloquial patois with a grating accent: *"Ne sois pas sainte nitouche... Don't be such a goody-goody."* Don't be a dead fly.

That night we went to one of the two bars in town, where the lady manager engaged in a promiscuous kind of democracy much to the chagrin of the neighbors who demanded the closure of the premises as well as the closing of the borders to blacks. Mrs. Martina had a prominent jaw and two red cheeks the size of peaches. The Vietnamese, Poles, Nigerians, Russians, and Turks were always greeted with the same phrase and the same cackle: "Here we drink beer. I don't care if the one who's thirsty is yellow, black, blue with red dots, or lilac with green freckles." It was in that place

where, darkly encouraged by something I was still
unable to specify exactly, I asked Estévez about Teresa
Clavel.

"Forget what you've heard," he said.

"Did you lie?"

Estévez almost killed me with his gaze. But in
keeping with his superbly generous disposition he
immediately said:

"It's not in your best interest to know."

I licked my lips in anticipation of the beer while
the barmaid was slicing off the foam with a brush.

"Do you know where she is?"

He paused dramatically enough to emphasize that
his response implied a gesture of trust toward me that
put our friendship on another level.

"Yes," he said sparingly.

One beer called for another, and, perhaps moved
by nostalgia for his beloved, and his long celibacy,
Estévez went into details about his erotic life, his voice
more hoarse than usual, and with a certain noble
objectivity alien to any coarseness.

According to his account, Teresa Clavel was a
woman of quick arousal, wonderfully moist, muscular,
with a sex that "molded" (he used that verb) as energetically as it was nimble to his own, lively and deep

with her tongue wherever she applied it, and in her endings: agonizing, gushing.

If in action she was someone capable of enjoying love in the way she either gave it or took it, in her quietude she was simply beautiful: her skin framed by her exuberant braided hair, her mouth wide and fruity, her neck soft and inquisitive, her hands reflective along her slightly bony cheekbones. She was sensitive and excited by both physical and intellectual games. Some words uttered with the reckless breathing beside her earlobes could drive her *insane* (he used that adjective).

Their conversation was impassioned. She followed his political activity with a certain poetic fervor that amused the realist Estévez, who, when he resisted her with pragmatic arguments, endured epithets of "yellow," soft, inconsequential, cynical. In any case, these disputes—Estévez sighed—melted away as much in bed as with their political action. Teresa Clavel could not come to see him in Switzerland, because she would have to leave Haiti clandestinely.

"And now forget what you've just heard."

"If you want me to forget it, why'd you tell me?"

He rubbed his hands over the etched glass of the beer mug.

279

"It's just that you're like..."

Estévez left the sentence unfinished. He thought that suspending it like that would be less hurtful. He made a little shrug with his shoulders as if apologizing for not being able to find the right word. I hated him. I hated him in minute detail. The virility of his voice, the magnetism of his gaze, the mustache that tinged his energetic lips, the contempt he felt for his sores, the lack of pathos with which he referred to his suffering in prison, the modesty with which he downplayed his exploits, the stoicism with which he let the days pass, the certainty of his political convictions that would lead him once again to the struggle against the dictatorship in his homeland and to Teresa Clavel's bed. I, on the other hand, was a master of apathy.

Evoking his beloved had depressed him. But nostalgia, instead of darkening his spirits, gave him the tenderness of a movie star, an air of warm sadness. The waitress approached him and said: "What's the matter, my love?" and Estévez smiled at her and ran his index finger first across the girl's cheek and then across her lips and inquiringly parted them with his finger, and the girl, changing her playful expression to a ceremonial one, stuck out her tongue and licked it.

I left the bar alone, humiliated by the drizzle. That I even cast a shadow on those narrow streets seemed strange to me. My skinny body felt electrified with furious emotion: I wanted to be in Estévez's place. I would have liked, in such haste, to put my own penis where he had made that incursion with his finger. I abhorred my anonymity. And the stupid shadow that was walking ahead of me, guiding me along the way to nowhere.

I envied Estévez so much that that night, alone in our room, while he was finding pleasure in the waitress, I resolved to make love to his Teresa Clavel.

At that moment I didn't know how much wickedness I was going to invest in that endeavor and the outcome I still hold on to not so much for the sake of narrative technique as for the shame I feel. Suffice it to say that the days passed with perfect irrelevance. German lessons from a caring, sentimental teacher, documentaries about the rivers and castles in the region, chess and Ping-Pong tournaments, photographs in profile, front and back, application signatures, waiting in line at the bank to receive our allowances.

Until one evening the asylum officer showed up at our room in a state of agitation.

"My heart is torn in two; I'm bringing you both good news and bad news." He rubbed his chin and took a deep breath. "The good news is for you, Mr. Estévez. The commission agreed to grant you asylum and to finance your stay in our country until you find...dignified...employment. The bad news is for you, Mr....?"

He rifled through his files in search of my last name, and I guessed what he was going to tell me. My modest imagination had not helped my skimpy record, and Estévez's generous reverie seemed suspicious to the bureaucrats. *Bref*: they had sent a fax to the Haitian minister of the interior with my background information, asking if there was anything against me, and the answer was in the file: "Absolutely nothing; interrogated and detained by the intelligence services as a matter of routine; honorable Haitian citizen; of good family; he is guaranteed full freedom and security throughout the country."

The Swiss authorities provided me with a plane ticket to Port-au-Prince and a nice sum of money that would allow me to buy cigarettes at the duty-free shop in the Zurich airport. Because the first flight wasn't until the next day, I was given that night to pack my things (the official looked at my two shirts hanging on the clothes rack), and then a few hours of reflection to see if I would decide to appeal the mandatory repatriation.

No doubt that I'm no hero, so when I told the official that I accepted my deportation without delay, it was because I was excited to make love sooner rather than later to Teresa Clavel.

I gathered my tickets, money, credentials, a brochure explaining the accommodations at the Zurich airport, and placed them on top of the miserable table. As for Estévez, the police transferred him to Bern. There were a number of international organizations there, offices hospitable to democratic ways of thinking. As a matter of reassurance, the policeman informed Estévez that his case file contained the opinion of the Swiss minister of foreign affairs, in which a ministry position for Estévez was predicted in a regime that would replace the dictatorship. He then gave me a casual look and filled me in on the details of my departure.

As soon as he left, I handed a pencil and paper to Estévez and told him, almost ordered him, to write to Teresa Clavel. I wanted to show him the extent of my friendship by doing him a favor, I wanted to prove to him that I was capable of one act of courage, and I wanted to place myself at his command for some mission in our homeland. I asked only that her name and address not appear at the top of the letter. I would memorize them. That would be his vote of confidence in me: his partner in captivity.

Estévez looked at his fingers and studied them as if he were holding a deck of cards between them that he could shuffle in different ways. Then he crisscrossed his fingers and cracked his knuckles. The man was trying to pin down what his intuition was telling him about me. The possibility of contacting Teresa Clavel excited him. The risk that I would sing of her where-abouts after a beating at the airport was holding him back. So I played my trump card.

"Forget it," I said, sounding offended.

He was a sort of guy with manly sentimentality. That a brother in captivity would betray him didn't enter into his universe. It was impossible to imagine that the cowardice he so rigorously disdained might reside in someone else. He put a hand on my left shoulder, squeezed it fraternally, and in the light of the indifferent bulb wrote feverishly.

When he had finished the page, he simply folded it in quarters and put it in my shirt pocket.

"Porte Verte," he added laconically.

I understood that this address could give me a passport to some dignity and identity that I lacked. The tender feeling that I was a recipient of his trust moistened my eyes and was at that moment sincere. That caused him to bring his hand up to my cheek and slap it with loving complicity.

As soon as the DC-10 reached cruising speed, I accepted a Cuba libre from the flight attendant and began to read the short message he had written on the notepaper. Estévez was obviously not a poet, but the cheesiness of his expressions did not conceal the genuine passion and the incredible precision of his feelings. The letter contained a paraphrase of Carl Brouard's Africanist poem that everyone learns in school: "Drum, when you sound, my soul howls for Africa." In Estévez's rough version: "Teresa, when my heart beats, it howls for you." That was his most tender lyrical moment in the letter. The rest, pure carnal literature: he described how cold his Swiss sheets were, the memory of her armpits under the sensitive taste buds on his broad tongue, the soothing warmth with which that same tongue ran over her gums, the intense memory of his own teeth biting the prominent sphere of "your little ass."

Excited, I gulped down the Cuba libre. "Estévez," I telegraphed from the clouds, "you've tied the dog up with sausages."

My fears of being sucked into the airport by the dictator's gendarmes vanished at passport control. The policemen, weary from humidity and hunger, let all the people of color pass through with a reluctant wave of their hands, *"Allez, allez."* Only white visitors were subjected to a computer check. The ousted Aristide was quite popular in North American religious circles and every pale face was presumed to be an activist opposing the dictator.

Once back in my apartment I looked through the telephone directory, searching for the Porte Verte address with a certain anticipatory bitterness that it had all been a clever misdirection by Estévez, cautious politician and connoisseur of spirit that he was. The location was listed in the directory. What was missing, however, was the telephone in my house. It had been cut away with a knife. A quick look at the closets and kitchen revealed that the rooms were considerably relieved of their contents. Only large items, the bed and refrigerator, for example, were still in place, but the door handles, the broom and duster, my Edith Piaf record collection had been taken, and of course the record player. In a very Haitian gesture of respect for culture, they had spared my books.

The goods I carried in my suitcase were more valuable than the detritus in my room. I used the razor, the fine cologne I bought in the duty-free shop, the turquoise silk shirt, the impeccable beige nappa pants, the white double-breasted jacket, which would have been entirely ironic to wear in Switzerland, and the lighter, from which I flipped a flame that led me to my tobacco and reflection while I looked out at the sleeping street. One cigarette led to another. Something told me that it was *convenient* to look for Teresa Clavel in the humid *patois* night, under the discretion of the moon and the loose bindings of tavern alcohol. Porte Verte was a bar far from the port, in the direction of the capital's wealthiest district. A place where the clandestine woman could take up her unsuspected residence.

How indifferent nature is to history! The night was impeccable: the stars balanced in the galaxy as if they made some sense, the moon opulent and revealing, the children dancing to rap music on the corners using only the clicking of their fingers snapping, and most of all the sea, restless like a curtain asking to be pulled back. The happiness of that breeze doubled with the cab window slightly open. At long last, I said to myself, this is my homeland. This moment. Homeland for me was the anticipation of my bare knee opening Teresa Clavel's thighs from behind.

The cab driver gave me a sly look in the rearview mirror when I paid and maintained his cheeky attitude for a while longer. He must have thought I had come back to my native land with European money, boastful clothes, and brothel cravings. Or maybe not. Perhaps, Porte Verte was already a warren known to Michel François and his cronies and the driver was an attaché who scoffed at my impending future in the dungeons. My own behavior never ceased to amaze me: instead of drinking the boisterous saliva of Teresa Clavel, perhaps that very night I would be buried in the excrement of the neo-Duvalierist heirs of the Tontons Macoutes.

At the bar I made sure the prostitutes understood that I was looking for something very precise and that their advances were futile. I had an appointment with a certain lady and I didn't want them breathing down my neck. The pianist's repertoire was typical of all the "elegant" bars in Petionville: "Feelings," "Me Olvidé de Vivir," "La Sombra de Tu Sonrisa," "Perfidia." When I ordered my second Cuba libre I signaled the lanky bartender to lean over.

"I have a message from Estévez," I told him. And I emphasized the importance of this information by pointing my thumb backward: "From Europe."

There's a moment in "seismic" countries where life and death hinge on a face and a stamp, a sigh, or a glance. A blink of an eye is all it takes to go from fraternal embrace to betrayal. Everything is hindrance. The waiter rubbed an already infinitely dry glass ad nauseam. He wouldn't look at me. I could almost feel how his saliva was cascading in a waterfall down his narrow pharynx.

"A message for Teresa Clavel," I added in a whisper.

If so far it had been his turn to be terrified, now it was mine. My game had fallen over the precipice and onto the counter. My happiness or my torment depended on the next few minutes. When the bartender walked toward the leading lady's dressing room in funereal silence, he might as well have left me at the disposal of some commando who would slice me up without any inhibitions. But, oh goddess of ambiguity, that man with a hand perfectly steady for shaking cocktails also had to tremblingly consider the fact that to my rear there might be an efficient platoon of riflemen ready to blow his brains out and maybe even the sensual skull of the beauty he was protecting.

There was another possibility: the craps one. That the seven would come up on the first play and we would all win. That I was indeed a messenger for Estévez and not an agent of Cedras, that he was in fact a democratic young man and not bait to hunt flaming dupes like me.

I do not recommend seismic uncertainty to anyone.

Tuned into the change of atmosphere in the cabaret, the pianist realized that he had to be quiet. The three female "companions," only moments before bulging their breasts and makeup, now looked like unerotic office workers wearing colorful miniskirts in the half light of the back table where they were sitting, allowing their adulterous bosses to grope them. I raised my glass with false aplomb and offered them a toast, a gesture that elicited not even the slightest reciprocation. I drank that local rum after rattling the ice cubes around like maracas, wearing the last smile of someone who has lost everything.

Later the bartender came over and stuck out his hand without saying anything. I took Estévez's letter out of my jacket and handed it to him. Bent, as if ten years of hitchhiking had fallen on his shoulders, the man returned to the dressing room, and now I could enjoy being, for the first time in my life, the center of attention in a public place.

I felt that same compelling strength in me, almost like the thickness of metal, as I held their glances, their silence. I equated that feeling with Estévez's way of being. He wasn't occasionally this magnetic. He was this way all the time. He was *professionally* the protagonist of his life. It was only my avaricious purpose, my vicarious fantasy, that gave me the possibility of living for one instant like a man.

Then the waiter ushered me into the dressing room. A false door opened behind the mirror. A hallway appeared. It led to a staircase. There the man stopped and told me to climb it. There were sacks of flour and corn everywhere. Instead of food stockpiles I thought of those barricades and trenches that are erected in gun battles. The steps led to a small room, a sort of cellar improvised to be a room, where Teresa Clavel, next to a floor lamp, was reading Estévez's flaming missive maybe for the fifth time.

My mouth filled up with spit. The way that clandestine light outlined her figure attached a magical touch to her sexuality, something I perceived as an artistic effect, the color degradation of Dutch painters, the melancholy of an American film from the forties. I didn't desire her any less. I coveted her even more and in a different way. Estévez, beleaguered by her countenance perhaps, had been rather impudent during that night of confessions, forgetting features on her face that gave a certain fickleness to her erotic energy. Her delicate jaw, her small ears, the lobes from which two small, cheap pearls sprouted, her nose a little softer than her dark mulatto lips.

"What's your name?" she asked.

My future infamy, the realistic analysis of my existence, my anonymity disguised as modesty, put these words in my mouth:

"I'm a friend of Estévez."

The woman waved the letter above the lamp and then came toward me.

"It's a very authentic letter," she said.

"Completely authentic."

"I'm referring to the content and not to the author."

"Me too."

"So you've read it."

"Absentmindedly."

She stood at a slight distance and kissed my cheeks three times.

"It takes courage to get this far."

"I wouldn't call it courage."

Inside the right pocket of my white jacket I clenched my knife. I touched the mechanism that made its blade pop out automatically.

"I love you, *madame*."

Teresa Clavel raised her chin and lowered her eyes and looked from my shoes to my forehead.

"Since we've never met, I imagine that your love for me is a symbol of your love for the cause."

"I like democracy, but I am basically indifferent to it. I've never been happy under any regime."

"So?"

"I wanted to tell you that I'm envious of Estévez's luck."

"You envy him? You have the good fortune to be living in your own country while he's in exile. Far from everything he loves."

"Far from you."

Without removing my right hand from my jacket pocket, I raised my left hand and with the back of it I gently stroked one of her cheeks. The woman's lips parted and her gaze became cautiously distant. I insisted on my light caress, until I brought one of my fingers to her lips, plunged it over her lower one, and immediately ran it over her eager little teeth. My longing... my *madness* was for her to slather it with her tongue, and for that minimal gesture to unleash our love. I was anticipating the delirium of my mouth filled with the juice of her sex. But the woman turned her lips away, soft and forceful.

"You're an asshole," she said.

"A consistent asshole," I said.

I pulled out the knife and the blade flared out right beside her neck.

She endured it in contempt. I squeezed her, plunged my hands down her ass cheeks, touched her breasts, bit them through the thin fabric of her red dress, laid her on the bed, pulled down her skimpy white panties, penetrated her, and in thirty seconds I was electric and convulsive on top of her. The woman pushed me away. She picked up Estévez's letter from the floor and went to the lamp and read it again. I hurried to zip up my pants and head out to the street. I hadn't even taken off my jacket.

I went back to my apartment in Senghor and let the days and nights go by living in that intemperate condition. I watched the military patrols pass by from my window and I was neither afraid nor interested. I bought a new telephone with the rest of the European money I had. I connected the line myself, and one day I dialed Estévez's phone in Geneva. I let it ring for a long time, but there was no answer.

In the community library in my neighborhood, the head librarian, a friend of my mother's, offered me a position in the English book section. A pointless job, since there were hardly any patrons. It should be noted that the salary was commensurate with the energy the job required. As an inveterately skinny guy, however, my expenses were mainly tobacco and rum.

Then pressures from the United States and the United Nations, which to my dwindling understanding are one and the same, forced the return of the ousted president to Haiti. It was news that neither concerned nor excited me. But adjacent to this bit of news was another one. In order to ensure a smooth transition, a man close to the president exiled in the U.S. would be appointed to a ministry position and would prepare for his return to Port-au-Prince: Robert Malval. Beneath a huge photo of him there was a no less extensive article announcing the return of a prominent group of exiles. Naturally, in portrait with suitcase about to depart, the first of them was Estévez.

I took stock of my life and the results were rather frugal. If a ministry awaited Estévez, for me it was tedium among books in a language I knew only from a few pop songs. If Teresa Clavel awaited Estévez, the comfort of my lonely sheets awaited me.

An escape by boat to Miami, frequent in those days, struck me as too risky, ambiguous, melancholic, and worst of all, no one could assure me that my life in the U.S. would be livelier than in Haiti.

I decided to stay. After about a week my apartment doorbell rang and I jumped out of bed to open the door to find Estévez. He had allowed his mustache to grow and his eyes had a hard and uncompromising look. He was holding a closed knife in his hand. He triggered the device at his hip and made the blade spring open.

"You left this at Teresa's house," he said.

Almost as if I were guessing, I wanted to bring my hand to my cheek to protect it. After a second I knew that it would be a useless gesture. Estévez scored a line on my cheek with his blade, from high on my cheekbone to the corner of my upper right lip. I felt the deep, hot gash and I fought the pain by gritting my teeth.

Then he put the knife on my bed, and in the frenzy of the bloodletting I noticed that the bedspread was stained with a red line. He interlocked his fingers and, in a gesture that was characteristic of him, he cracked his knuckles. He spent a few seconds reluctantly observing my riotous blood, and certainly satisfied with his task, he headed for the door. There he put his hands in his pockets to emphasize his indifference.

"This is as far as it goes, because if I kill you, your name might very well appear in the papers tomorrow."

borges

*Our nothingness differs little; it is a trivial
and fortuitous coincidence that you are the
reader of these exercises, and I their author.*

JORGE LUIS BORGES
Fervor de Buenos Aires

F ed up with my loneliness, I decided to travel. I called Miguel in Buenos Aires, but he didn't answer his phone.

I dialed Tomás's number in Argentina and he told me that Miguel had left with Natalie. "*Il est à Paris,*" he quipped. "He wants to be a big deal in France."

I bought a plane ticket to Paris with the credit card a bank manager had unwisely offered me, and I hung a map of the world on a wall in my empty apartment

and traced the route from Chile to Europe with a red
pencil. My desolation was as vast as that sea separat-
ing the continents.

I looked through my address book for the phone
numbers of friends I could say goodbye to. Then I
decided not to bother them. Who really cared about
my fate if I suffered from the melancholy of a wifeless
man: always the last one to leave social gatherings
by the time cigarette butts and red wine stained the
tablecloth?

I infected everything with my melancholy. One
day I overcame my shyness and asked the waitress
at a restaurant out on a date. I even bought an electric toaster so I could make her a nice breakfast the
following morning. But she never showed up. She gave
no explanation either. I went to the place where she
worked but she wasn't there.

I dialed Susana's number. At one point we'd talked
about finding a place and living together. But I made
the awkward mistake of falling in love with her. That,
she told me, changed everything. She wasn't at all
stunned by my impending departure. She asked me
to buy a particular perfume she liked at the duty-free
shop on my way back. Why did she assume I'd be

coming back? Everyone seemed to associate me with mediocre projects.

The in-flight magazine on the plane included a psych evaluation. The last question was: "What is the most defining feature of your personality?" The unchanging Argentine pampa stretched out below me. "Availability," I wrote. I added and subtracted points and arrived at my psychogram: "You are a person lacking convictions, noncommunicative and apathetic. Make an effort to break out of your confinement."

"Exactly," I said to myself. I was on my way to Paris.

I'd call Miguel and he'd invite me to stay at his apartment. He'd been involved with Natalie for a while now. She was French and went to Buenos Aires to write a thesis on Borges. Miguel met her outside a movie theater. He convinced her that he was better than Borges. Only thing was that he had published just one book. They became lovers and Natalie started writing her thesis on Miguel's novel: *Country Without Borders*.

My friendship with Miguel began with the same book. When he published it, ten copies were sent to Chile. I wrote an engrossing review in a weekly where

I was a contributor and readers bought up the limited stock in a matter of days. Having heard about the impact of my review from the bookseller, Miguel offered me his "eternal" friendship and his gratitude.

He had always wanted to go to Paris. "Here the shadow of Borges is too vast." Years earlier I had given up on the idea of being a poet on the other side of the Andes, because of Neruda's shadow.

*

At Charles de Gaulle I experienced a pleasant few minutes of excitement. I was in the city of my dreams, in the inner sanctum of my favorite films. Here I would find a girl with pale skin, brown hair, and an old gray raincoat, like the violinist who is snubbed by the businessman in *Shoot the Piano Player*.

The bus ride to the city gradually chipped away at my enthusiasm. Every city has its routine, just as every soul does. To assuage my sudden depression I drank a café au lait in the bus terminal and called Miguel from the pay phone, almost certain that I wasn't going to reach him.

When I told him who I was, he asked for my last name. It irritated me to learn that he had other acquaintances who shared the same first name as me. He then repeated my first and last name; he sounded crestfallen.

I immediately told him that I'd go to a hotel.

He wouldn't allow it. I was one of his closest friends. I had to stay in his home. Although I had come at a very special moment. "Very special," he repeated. I took a cab and was startled by the velocity at which the fare increased block by block. Some women crossed the streets with baguettes under their arms. It was an overwhelmingly beautiful city, but the French walked quickly as if they weren't aware of it.

The building's doorman gave me a grim look. He didn't know how to pronounce Miguel's name and reluctantly identified his apartment. He made no move to help me with my suitcase either. He glanced at the duty-free bag in the elevator. I'd already bought Susana's perfume and a bottle of scotch. The doorman looked at the bottle and said something I didn't understand.

When Miguel opened the door he looked pale and disheveled. Debris and wreckage were lying scattered in piles around him: a crushed mirror on the parquet floor, feathers from the armchair, and, on the table, the knife that had been used to slash it.

He hugged me, held me in an apologetic embrace, pressing his cheek into my beard.

"Natalie left me. She told me that if she didn't leave me she was going to kill me."

"I can see that," I muttered.

A sudden breeze drew my gaze to the large window. It had been shattered by some blunt object that had probably fallen to the street.

I thought it prudent to take the bottle of scotch out of the plastic bag and put it on the table. I was about to set it down but I saw that the glass top was also broken. When Miguel opened the bottle and brought two Bakelite cups from the bathroom, I surmised that the glassware had also perished in the scuffle.

We toasted without saying anything and even poured ourselves another shot in silence. Then he opened the door to a small room.

"This is the guest room."

"I can go to a hotel."

"That's not necessary. I think I'll spend a little time in the bathroom now. I need to cry."

"You can do that here. You're my friend."

But he disappeared down the hallway and almost immediately I thought I heard water running. There was a knock on the front door and I opened it. It

was the doorman. He was holding an iron bust of
Borges.

"Someone threw this into the courtyard," he said.

*

As I poured myself another scotch, I spotted a portrait
of Natalie on the nightstand. The image must have
been around four years old, from about the time I
visited her apartment in Buenos Aires. As I watched
them cooking pasta together and discussing something
trivial I'd decided that she was the girl I was looking
for. A partner like Natalie, who would talk on the
phone with her closest friends while I grated Parmesan
cheese in the kitchen to drizzle over the ravioli. Out of
all the women who had never in their lives loved me,
she was the one who excited me the most. She was the
only person I ever told that when I was ten years old,
my mother was dragged from our house at dawn and I
never saw her again. I don't know why I told her, since
everyone has me pegged as taciturn. That is, even in
the midst of the detritus of that apartment, Natalie's
photo alone summoned something wider and richer
than that space in ruins. I knocked on the bathroom
door.

"I'm okay," Miguel said. "Don't worry about me."

But he didn't open the door. The water was still running over the bathroom sink. I imagined he was watching it escape through the drain without fixing his mind on any particular point. I went back to the living room. I stopped in front of a pearly blue manuscript box with lettering on the side that read "novel." I removed the contents and went through them quickly, flipping through the pages with my thumb. It was a ream of five hundred sheets but no more than fifteen had writing on them. The others were blank. More than blank, I thought, they were empty. I put them back in the box and looked at the phone. I sat down with the plastic cup in my hands and let time pass.

Then Miguel came out of the bathroom, approached me, and put a hand on my shoulder.

"How are things in Chile?"

I shrugged. Once again the breeze came through the cracks in the window and Miguel drew the curtains. It got really dark. The living room overlooked an inner courtyard, a kind of light well, though even at noon there were long shadows.

"As you can see," he said to me, lighting a table lamp, "this is *Paris c'est fini*."

"Is it definite?"

"She told me that if she didn't leave she was going to kill me."

"What are you going to do?"

"Go back to Buenos Aires."

"Borges is dead." I smiled softly.

He looked down at the box where his novel was and I looked away, at Natalie's portrait. I thought of the world map nailed to my apartment wall in Santiago and the furious red lines I had drawn across the ocean. Just as a cartographer reduces distances to tiny proportions, so too had my life been reduced.

"Help me pack," Miguel said with sudden anguish. I grabbed his arm, stopping him.

"Have another drink. You can think about that later, when you're calmer."

He looked at the bottle on the table and rubbed his cheeks hard. I realized at that moment he was wearing a polka-dot tie with the knot perfectly centered on his starch-soaked collar.

"Decisions," he said. "It's important to act so that it doesn't hurt."

"Believe me, I understand," I said, looking at my own unopened suitcase.

"The world comes and goes," he said. "What brought you to France?"

Answering "You" and saying "Natalie" seemed foolish. Inside my jacket I had a copy of a Chilean current affairs magazine with a soldier on the cover.

"A story," I said. "My magazine sent me here for a story."

"Literary?"

"Yes. Literary," I said.

"You know Kundera lives here, right?"

He went to his room for his suitcase and put it down on the center of the table. On the next trip he brought suits, meticulously folded shirts, well-shined shoes, socks in springy rolls. He covered everything with a Maigret-style raincoat. He called the airport. He wanted to know if there was a flight that same night. He said, "Window seat."

"I'm a terrible host," he said, combing his temples with his hands. "If she stays she'll kill me. If I stay here alone I'll die."

"If I were you I'd sleep on it. Buenos Aires is a long way away."

"I've already made the reservation."

"You can cancel it."

He looked at the half-empty bottle.

"Do you want me to fix you something to eat?"

"No, thanks."

"An omelet."

"No need." He swept up a few pieces of glass and piled them next to the doormat.

He put on his jacket and extracted a ring of keys from his pocket. He gathered a few last items from the apartment and shook his head, as if he couldn't believe what he was seeing. He put the key ring in my hand.

"It's your house now," he said.

I played with the keys, shaking them in my fist, showing him my confusion.

"But what am I supposed to do? The rent, the telephone..."

"I'll call you about those details."

He hugged me and then slapped me gently on the cheek. A lot of Argentines used to do that.

"You'll see that Paris is a marvelous city."

"Without a doubt."

"A city to be happy in."

He picked up a huge piece of broken glass with his hand and placed it with the others next to the doormat.

We hugged each other again and he went out to the street to catch a cab. I took a long look at the apartment keys in my hand and then placed them

on the table next to the bottle of scotch. That heavy
fatigue that comes from crossing an ocean rose into
my eyelids. I stopped in front of the small guest room
with its perfectly made bed and a mediocre Botero
reproduction over the headboard. That asepsis
reminded me of furnishings in Santiago.

I wandered into the master bedroom.

The mattress had been slashed in several places
and feathers and springs sprouted out of different
spots across its surface. The sheet had spilled onto the
carpet along with teacups and slices of black bread. I
grabbed it and, rather impulsively, I breathed its scent
in deeply. I was disturbed by my memory of Natalie.
One cold night in Buenos Aires I had borrowed a
white cashmere sweater impregnated with that scent.

I tucked my arm under the pillow, a habit I've had
since I was a child, and covered myself with the sheet
all the while continuing to breathe it in.

Gradually it became dark and the curtains fluttered, moved by the air seeping through the cracks. I
turned on the lamp and then went to the living room
and tried to stop the gusts of wind by taping a couple of pages of *Le Figaro* onto what remained of the
window. Then I sank into the armchair and thought
about my involvement in something that ought to

matter to me: my own life. I concluded that I had made, as in a game of chess, a perfect check castling out of nothingness. I had moved my entire helplessness from Chile to France. The only one who would benefit from my trip was going to be Susana with her little bottle from duty-free.

*

I wasn't hungry, and I wasn't in the mood to visit the possible havoc in the kitchen. I desperately wanted a cup of coffee, but I didn't get up from the armchair.

Then I heard a key being inserted into the lock and the violent light from the hall rushed over my body. Natalie was standing in the doorframe, paler than in my memory, fixed in that black corduroy coat. She flipped on the light switch and kept her gaze on me, trying to shift from surprise to recognition.

"Natalie, don't you remember me?"

She put her hands to her cheeks and her teeth sprang out from behind her smile.

"But you're the Chilean!"

She came over to hug me and then she didn't seem to know what to do with her hands.

"What are you doing in Paris?"

"I came to write an article."

311

"What about?"

"About Kundera. About Milan Kundera."

Natalie took off her coat and threw it over the armchair. She was wearing a moss-green turtleneck sweater and a black leather miniskirt. My eyes moved from her knees to her blue eyes, her eyelids heavy with makeup the same shade as her sweater and her eyelashes thick with a paste that gave her a certain vintage-film look.

"How do I look?"

I stared at her feet, in those moments when she was taking off her shoes, she was becoming smaller, more vulnerable.

"Absolutely stunning," I said.

Then she looked down the hall and ran to the bedroom. She came back, her neck sinking into her sweater, stretching it out as if she were short of breath.

"Where is Miguel?"

I moved toward her and squeezed her hands gently.

"He left."

"When is he coming back?"

"He went to Buenos Aires, Natalie."

She grabbed the pack of cigarettes off the table and I rushed over to light one for her. She tossed her hair back with a dramatic gesture. She exhaled the smoke, and then she crossed her arms. With the big toe of her bare foot she nudged a piece of glass gently.

"So, *Paris c'est fini*," she said humorlessly.

"He said the same thing."

She walked over to the telephone and checked to make sure there was a dial tone. She put it back on the cradle.

"All of this," she raised her arms, encompassing much more than the space in that living room, "is a shipwreck. An immense and immeasurable shipwreck."

She opened the door to the guest room and saw that my suitcase was on the bed.

She removed it and straightened the blanket with both hands as she held the cigarette between her lips. She spoke to me without taking it out of her mouth.

"You must be dead tired."

"More like confused."

"It will do you good to sleep. Do you want something to eat?"

"I'm not hungry."

She stroked the back of her neck as if she wanted to remember something, but in the end said nothing. I brought the whiskey back to the room and poured another shot into the plastic cup. I went to the kitchen to look for ice.

Through the half-open bathroom door I saw Natalie looking at herself in the mirror. I went back to my room, lay down, and put the keys on the bedside table. I fell asleep looking at them.

*

I woke up feeling hungry and in an unfamiliar mood. I opened my suitcase and took out my favorite shirt and sweater. I put them on energetically and, finding no container for my dirty laundry in the room, I stuffed it under the bed.

I went into the living room and saw Natalie sleeping, curled up in the armchair with the phone pressed to her ear. She had taken off her leather miniskirt and with her sweater pulled up over her bare waist I could see a large part of her white slip with fretwork where the shadow of her pubis was sharply visible. Although the heater was working, the wind, coming through the window inadequately covered by the newspaper, had lowered the temperature. I brought the blanket from my room and draped it over her.

I picked up the key ring decisively and stepped out into the Parisian morning, letting my instinct lead me so as not to expose myself to the hostilities of passersby while asking them for directions.

I bought a long golden baguette at the bakery and even before I paid for it I couldn't help biting off the tip. I wandered around with the bread for a couple of blocks, until I found a glazier's shop. My body was reflected in the dozens of mirrors on sale in the window and I felt like someone else, with that bread in my hand and my hair disheveled.

I gave the clerk the building address and made an appointment for an hour later.

Back in the apartment I went to the kitchen, cut the bread into generous slices, plunged the tea bags into the boiling water, and placed portions of butter, cheese, and ham on a platter, along with a bunch of grapes. A ray of sunlight fell dissolvingly on the kitchen tablecloth and in that light the breakfast took on the hue of a hyperrealistic painting.

Only after the tea gave off its strong color in the emerald cups and the smoke melded with the sun's dust, only then did I go to Natalie and wake her by touching her cheek.

She sat up in the armchair with a start and picked up the telephone receiver. She checked for a dial tone and only then extended her hand for me to shake.

"*Bonjour*," she said.

I invited her into the kitchen. The light had taken possession of the space. Now there was a suggestion of intimacy that the other rooms lacked. She cheered my gastronomic offering, with a Parisian *Ooh la la*, and then folded herself into the chair with her slender legs curled under her on the cushion. Thus, almost naked, polished with failure, she seemed to me even more beautiful than in Buenos Aires.

I drank my tea holding the cup with both hands and close to my face. In that silence I could hear her little teeth crunching a piece of baguette garnished with a slice of ham.

"After breakfast I'll take a shower and go to a hotel," I said.

She swallowed quickly and shook her head before she could speak.

"That's not necessary. There's the guest room."

I moved some crumbs around on the table: with the edge of one hand I swept them into the hollow of the other. Then I licked them with my tongue and swallowed them.

We sipped another cup of tea, circling around something vague. I fumbled around, touching my shirt, and couldn't find the pack of cigarettes.

"I feel like smoking, too," she said, moving as if to stand and get the cigarettes from the living room.

I stopped her by placing a hand on her forehead.

"I'll go. Don't get up," I said.

She hugged herself and rubbed her own shoulders.

"They're in my bag. There's an unopened pack."

I went to the living room and to add a little more light I tore off the newspaper that was covering the window. Any moment the glazier would show up with the new glass. I opened her black leather bag next to her miniskirt and reached inside for the tobacco. My fingers brushed against a metal object. I thought it might be a lighter, but when I grabbed it with my whole hand I saw that it was a revolver. I lifted it up and felt its full volume by weighing it in my right hand. It wasn't a "female" pistol. It was a weapon of modern size and design. I plunked it back into the bag and went to the kitchen with the cigarettes. As she lit hers she briefly covered the back of my hand with her right hand to protect the match flame. I lit mine and we both exhaled sharply and stood watching the smoke melt into the dust floating on the sunlight.

Then Natalie brought her face forward and, resting her elbows on the table, held her chin between both hands right in the middle of the mingled filigrees of smoke, sun, and tea steam.

"What do you say? Are you staying?" she asked.

I drew hard a second time, inhaled deeply, and wiped away a speck of tobacco that had stuck to my lip.

"Yes," I said.

antonio skármeta is a Chilean author who wrote the
novel that inspired the 1994 Academy Award–winning movie
Il Postino: The Postman. His fiction has received dozens of awards
and has been translated into nearly thirty languages. In 2011 his
novel *The Days of the Rainbow* (Other Press 2013) won the prestigious
Premio Iberoamericano Planeta-Casa de América de Narrativa.
His play *El Plebiscito* was the basis for the Oscar-nominated film *No*.

curtis bauer is a poet and translator of prose and poetry
from Spanish. He is the recipient of a PEN/Heim Translation
Fund Grant and a Banff International Literary Translation Centre
fellowship. His translation of Jeannette Clariond's *Image of Absence*
won the International Latino Book Award for Best Nonfiction Book
Translation from Spanish to English. Bauer teaches creative writing
and comparative literature at Texas Tech University.